Constrained laughter caught Rachel's attention, and she looked up. Across the room, Josh held the audience captivated as he talked.

She sighed. He looked handsome in his dark navy suit and tie—more like he belonged in a boardroom than out fighting fires. He stood tall and carried himself with a confidence she envied. He was a part of these people. He belonged here.

A young boy moved to stand beside Josh. She momentarily wiped away the numb ambivalence that had taken hold of her as she watched. Rachel's heart pounded as she looked from the boy to Josh and back to the boy. Even as Josh put his arm around the child and hugged him, Rachel realized that this child with his light-colored hair and expressive eyes could only be Josh's son.

Josh had a son.

TERRI REED

grew up in a small town nestled in the foothills of the Sierra Nevada. To entertain herself, she created stories in her head, and when she put those stories to paper, her teachers in grade school, high school and college encouraged her imagination. Living in Italy as an exchange student whetted her appetite for travel, and modeling in New York, Chicago and San Francisco gave her a love for the big city, as well. She has also coached gymnastics and taught in a preschool. She enjoys walks on the beach, hikes in the mountains and exploring cities. From a young age she attended church, but it wasn't until her thirties that she really understood the meaning of a faith-filled life. Now living in Portland, OR, with her college-sweetheart husband, two wonderful children, a rambunctious Australian shepherd and a fat guinea pig, she feels blessed to be able to share her stories and her faith with the world. She loves to hear from readers at P.O. Box 19555 Portland, OR 97280.

LOVE
COMES HOME

TERRI REED

STEEPLE HILL BOOKS

Steeple Hill®

ISBN 0-373-87268-2

LOVE COMES HOME

Copyright © 2004 by Terri Reed

www.SteepleHill.com

Printed in U.S.A.

"For I know the plans I have for you,"
declares the Lord, "plans for welfare and not for
calamity, to give you a future and a hope."
—*Jeremiah* 29:11

I want to dedicate this book
to everyone who has struggled to pursue a dream.
Keep believing. Faith and perseverance do pay off.

There are so many people to thank, who,
in one way or another, have touched my life
as a writer. I apologize if I've forgotten anyone
and ask for your forgiveness.

First and foremost, thank you to my husband and
children. I could never have done this without your
love and support. Thank you to my mother-in-law
for urging me to follow my dream. Thank you to
my mother for always believing in me.

A big thanks to my critique partners, Leah Vale and
Lissa Manley, for encouraging me, challenging me
to grow and never letting me quit.

Thank you to my writerly friends:
Melissa McClone, Delilah Ahrendt,
Tina Bilton-Smith, Amy Danicic, Carolyn Zane,
Susan Alverson, Cynthia Rutledge
and Lenora Worth. I have learned
and grown from knowing you.

And a heartfelt thanks to my spirit-filled sisters
who've been my cheering section as well as my
friends: Tricia, Sherry B., Sheri S., Deanna, Debbie
and all the ladies at Southlake Foursquare Church.
But mostly, I thank my Savior Jesus,
for all the blessings.

Chapter One

"For I know the plans I have for you," declares the Lord, "plans for welfare and not calamity, to give you a future and a hope."
—*Jeremiah* 29:11

She was home.

Inhaling deeply the fresh scent of pine and exhaust-free air, Dr. Rachel Maguire stared at the seven-story redbrick building, the words Sonora Community Hospital spelled out in bright blue letters across the side. A strange tightness pulled at her chest. As a child, this had been the first hospital she'd ever entered.

Her gaze dropped to another set of letters above the door in front of her. Her breath froze. The emergency entrance.

She shied away from using the double sliding doors, and instead followed the tidy walkway, carpeted on either side by lush green lawns, leading to the main entrance. The early-June sun warmed her face, and from high in the branches of a towering pine an unseen bird chirped a melodic tune. Off in the distance to the east, the peaks of the Sierra Nevadas rose to meet the clear blue sky. Even to her untrained eye, the vibrant greens and hues of brown and gold dotting the hillside were a painter's dream.

She paused, alert to the eerie peacefulness and serenity around her. With no outside noise to blend with, the unsettled, restless feelings she constantly lived with clamored for attention. She closed her eyes and willed the chaos to subside. She missed the pulsing beat of Chicago.

But not returning to California hadn't been an option.

Mom G. needed her.

Rachel took a deep breath, adjusted her grip on her small suitcase and walked through the sliding doors of the main hospital entrance. Even inside the hospital, tranquillity reigned. People waiting in the lobby area spoke in lowered tones and soothing, classical music played from somewhere overhead. She stepped briskly up to the administration desk.

"I'm looking for Mrs. Olivia Green's room."

The woman behind the desk smiled. "Hello, Rachel."

"Hello." She struggled to put a name to the round, wide-eyed face.

"Polly Anderson, now Campbell. You were a year ahead of me in school."

"Oh." Rachel didn't remember her, but smiled politely. "Hello, Polly."

"Your mom is on the fifth floor, room six. She'll be glad to see you. Welcome home."

Rachel blinked, surprised that anyone here would remember her after all this time and that there would be such open friendliness. Her fast-paced world had little time for niceties.

"Thank you, Polly," she said, and hurried to catch the elevator.

The doors opened on the fifth floor. Emotionally steeling herself, she stepped out. With a purposeful stride, she headed down the corridor. Overhead, the fluorescent lights glowed bright. A distinctive, familiar antiseptic smell assaulted her senses and settled in the back of her throat, offering her a measure of comfort.

Strange, she'd never before noticed how the quiet hum and soft beeping of machines coupled with the rumble of hushed voices lent the air a surreal quality. She'd spent so many years working in hospitals that her senses had grown accustomed to the surroundings. She couldn't remember ever noticing the atmosphere of her work. It was all part of being a doctor.

Only, this wasn't her hospital and she wasn't here as a doctor. She was a visitor. A chill ran down her spine. Someone she loved lay in one of these rooms. Even though she'd reviewed Mom G.'s chart and knew her prognosis, the older woman's condition didn't seem real. Rachel didn't want it to be real.

She stopped. Her breathing turned shallow. A long-suppressed memory surfaced, and her mind reeled. Memories of walking down a similar corridor. She'd been six years old, her hand held firmly in the grasp of Nurse Claire, the woman who'd taken charge of her after they'd arrived at the hospital.

"Is my mommy all right?"

The woman's kind gaze regarded her steadily. "I don't know, honey."

Not much comfort there. There'd been no daddy to

run to, either. After her mother had died, no man had come forward claiming her as his daughter. No one had wanted her.

Until years later, when her foster mother, Olivia Green, legally adopted her. But she'd insisted that Rachel keep her last name in honor of her mother.

Mom G. gave Rachel not only a place to belong but reason to hope. The generous woman's loving nature had stirred up Rachel's pain of losing her mother. And Rachel had finally given in to the tears she'd held so long. In her gentle wisdom, Mom G. had suggested Rachel channel her grief into making a difference in the world.

God had handed her a purpose in that moment. She would become a doctor so she could improve and change the triage techniques used in emergency rooms, procedures that had cost her mother her life. That was Rachel's life goal, her focus, never to be forgotten nor sidetracked from.

She squared her shoulders and continued walking.

Standing outside of room 6, she whispered, "Lord, I need Your strength."

When she pushed open the door, the fragrant scent of gardenias greeted her and she smiled, pleased to know the flowers she'd ordered had arrived. She wanted Mom G. to be surrounded by the things she loved.

Rachel stepped inside the cheery private room, her gaze taking in the woman she loved so dearly. She'd seen thousands of patients hooked up to IVs, heart rate and blood pressure monitors, and machines that helped the body function, but seeing the once-vibrant and beautiful Olivia Green hooked up accordingly made Rachel's knees wobbly. She quelled the uncharacteristic sensation by sheer will. She wouldn't give in to any weakness.

Remember your purpose.

But she hated seeing Mom G. so still and quiet. Rachel's gaze swung to the monitors. Heart rate, steady. Blood pressure, within a reasonable range.

Then her mind focused on the complete picture. A man sat beside the bed holding one of Mom G.'s hands. His bent head caused his tawny hair to fall forward over his brow. Dark blond lashes rested against bronze skin. His mouth moved with silent words.

Rachel swallowed. Agitated butterflies performed a riotous dance in the pit of her stomach. She blinked several times, hoping the man would disappear.

Josh Taylor. What was he doing here?

As though he'd heard her question, he opened his eyes and lifted his head. Their gazes locked. A smoldering blaze ignited and heat shimmered between them. Rachel drew in a cooling breath. She wouldn't allow this man to burn her again.

He slowly stood, his towering frame dwarfing the room.

Emotions churned and bubbled like a whirlpool inside her. They moved like running water through her consciousness so quickly she couldn't grasp one long enough to use as a defense against his presence. Her pulse leapt with unexpected pleasure, her heart ached with the sting of rejection and her cheeks flamed with sudden anger. She wasn't ready for this—for seeing Josh, feeling emotions she'd long ago buried. She hated being vulnerable and unsure.

So she did what had become natural—she cloaked herself in professionalism. She was a doctor. She'd come to help Mom G., not stir the embers of a past love.

She inclined her head. "Josh."

He followed suit. "Rachel." His deep voice brushed over her, making her shiver with surprising awareness.

Uncomfortable with her response, she set her suitcase by the door and went to the bed, focusing her attention on Mom G. Her color looked good. Rachel picked up a hand. Veins showed through the near translucent skin. Warm. Her hands were still warm. So many times Mom G.'s gentle hands had wiped a tear, clapped at an accomplishment, held hers when she needed comfort.

"I'm surprised to see you here, Rachel." Josh's softly spoken words broke the silence.

She lifted her gaze to his intense, gold-specked eyes and cocked her head to one side. "Why?"

"I never thought you'd come back."

His comment stung. "She needs me."

Josh nodded, his expression closed. "She does." He shrugged. "Still, I didn't really think you'd come."

Hurt burrowed in deep. Her spine straightened. "I guess that says a lot about what you think of me."

"You have no idea what I think of you."

The look in his vibrant gaze caught her off guard. If she didn't know better, she'd swear that beneath the disdain, she saw longing. But that couldn't be. Not after what had happened. He'd made his feelings clear years ago. With a mental tug she pulled her protective cloak tighter around her heart.

She pursed her lips. "You're right, Josh. I have no

idea what you think of me. And I'd just as soon keep it that way.''

''So would I.'' His expression hardened. ''So would I.''

What he thought of her didn't matter. Not in the least. What they'd had once was long over.

Ignoring his overwhelming presence and the commotion going on inside her, she picked up the chart hanging behind the bed and studied the notes. She clenched her teeth as she read. Mom G.'s condition had worsened in the last twenty-four hours. They'd prescribed Mannitol, a drug meant to prevent herniation of the brain stem, an extreme complication of a glioblastoma multiforme.

Josh shifted, drawing her attention. ''What's that say?''

She quickly looked away, avoiding his intent gaze, and replaced the chart. ''What have they told you about her condition?''

Josh let out a weary breath. ''She has a brain tumor with a long, fancy name. They operated but couldn't remove the full mass because of the risk of complications. Dr. Kessler said she's deteriorating rapidly and time's short.''

Rachel didn't want to hear those words, wouldn't allow her mind to register such dire news. A flush of anger ran through her. Dr. Kessler shouldn't have said that to Josh. The doctor shouldn't have ruled out hope.

''Yes, well.'' She glanced down at Mom G. Fear stabbed at her, making her edgy. ''We'll see about that.''

She wasn't about to give up. They'd barely started the chemotherapy, and other treatment options had yet to be explored. She'd find a way to help Mom G. She had to.

"She'll be happy to see you when she wakes up."

"How long has she been asleep?"

"She was sleeping when I arrived. And that was about thirty minutes before you. Why?"

Rachel kept the little burst of panic in check. Just because Mom G. lay sleeping didn't mean anything other than she was tired. The rational side of Rachel's brain warned that when the type of tumor Mom G. developed became severe enough, sleepiness eventually led to coma, then death. Rachel's emotional side that deeply loved her adoptive mother refused to acknowledge the information. "We should wake her."

"You should ask the doctor."

She bristled. "I *am* a doctor."

"But not *her* doctor," he gently reminded.

She couldn't refute that, though she was licensed to practice in the state of California as well as several other states. Her teaching schedule required traveling and being hands-on in other E.R.s around the country. But out of respect for Mom G.'s doctor, she said, "I'll go find Dr. Kessler."

Josh stepped around the bed and placed a hand on her arm. "You stay. I'll go find him."

Moved by his thoughtfulness, Rachel stared at his big, tanned hand where it rested against the lightweight blue fabric of her suit coat. Through the thin material, his warmth seeped into her skin. The touch evoked memories of younger days. Days when they'd been happy and in love, walking the school halls, side by side, Josh's arm casually draped about her shoulders or their fingers intertwined.

Days long gone.

"All right." Anything to create distance between them.

Josh moved past her. His long legs carried him with confidence. As the door swung shut behind him, the room suddenly seemed lonely and cold even though the warmth of the sun streamed through the window. She rubbed her arm where his touch lingered and went to the chair where he'd sat. Mom G. still slept. Rachel gathered one of the older woman's hands in her own and with the other hand smoothed back a faded blond curl. "Oh, Mom G., I'm so sorry this is happening to you. But I'm here now. I'll take care of you."

Oh, God. Please show me how to help her.

Unlike the doctors who couldn't save her mother, Rachel would do *anything* for Mom G. Even if that meant dealing with Josh, who was the last person she needed in her life. She had no intention of allowing the pain of the past to repeat itself.

"Sure thing, Josh." Dr. Kessler set the chart in his hand down on the counter of the nurses' station. "I'll speak with her right now."

"Thank you, Doctor." Josh liked the man and Mrs. G. trusted him.

Dr. Kessler stuck a pen into the breast pocket of his white coat. "Are you coming?"

"No. I'm going to get some coffee." He wasn't ready to see Rachel again just yet. Being near her, able to touch her, hear her voice after all these years had brought back so many memories of when they were teens. It was too much to deal with in such a short time.

As Dr. Kessler disappeared into the elevator, Josh

headed for the hospital chapel. He slipped into a pew. The quiet serenity of the room eased some of the turmoil within.

Almost twelve years. Twelve years since she'd walked out of his life, choosing her career, her dream of being a doctor, over their love—his love.

I love you, Josh, but I can't stay. I have to do this.

As he ran a hand through his thick hair, jagged pain engulfed him. Pain as fresh now as it had been then. As it had been when he was fourteen and his mother's words to his father mirrored Rachel's.

Sharon Taylor had decided being a mother and wife wasn't fulfilling enough. She'd left to pursue a career in the art world and never came back. She'd tried to contact Josh, had wanted to see him, but at fourteen, he'd been too hurt, too angry to welcome her overtures. He'd hardened his heart to her and refused to listen when his father tried to talk to him about her. Josh could never accept his father's claim that he'd loved her enough to let her go. After a time she'd stopped trying. And Josh tried to forget her.

It seemed the Taylor men were under a curse. Destined to love women who had no use for marriage, commitment or family.

Josh prayed fervently that when the time came, his son would find love with a woman committed to her family. A woman passionate about marriage and motherhood.

A woman nothing like Rachel Maguire.

He closed his eyes and rubbed his forehead.

He'd forced his feelings for Rachel aside and moved on with his life. He'd married and had a son whom he loved beyond anything he thought possible.

Josh opened his eyes and glanced at his watch.

School would let out soon. He hoped Griff remembered Grandpa was picking him up today. If he took the bus home, no one would be there. Thankfully Mrs. G's surgery and subsequent critical condition hadn't happened a week later since summer vacation would start on Monday.

Until her sickness, Mrs. G. had watched Griff after school. But when Mrs. G. had gone into the hospital, Josh had made it a point to be home from work when his son got there. But today, with Mrs. G.'s condition so critical, he needed to be at the hospital.

And now Rachel was here, too.

So much the same, yet so different. The once-pretty teen had grown into a beautiful woman. Her shoulder-length ebony hair framed her face and made the most of her startling blue eyes. He drew in a deep breath and could have sworn her scent clung to his clothes. She still smelled of a flowered meadow on a summer's day. Fresh, alive and invigorating.

That's what had first alerted him to her presence in the hospital room. The familiar and alluring scent of Rachel.

Contrary to what he'd said, he'd known she would return. He just hadn't realized how hard seeing her again would be. All the agony of having loved and lost, which he'd hidden away, was simmering and working its way through his heart. He didn't like it one bit.

He didn't need to remind himself that he wasn't enough, that his love wasn't enough. The knowledge was branded across his soul.

Yet this Rachel was different. As a teen she'd been warm and lively, full of laughter. Now she was so calmly cool and in control. She was like an exquisitely designed ice sculpture. Each angle and curve perfectly cut, the sleek and smooth surface beckoning to be touched. Yet to the one who dared, the scar of freezer burn would be their reward. This Rachel wasn't the woman he'd fallen in love with all those years ago. He took comfort in that. Finally something that didn't remind him of the past.

Staring up at the window, he watched sunlight splinter through the various colors of the beautiful stained-glass cross. He wanted to pray for himself, wanted to lay his troubles at the feet of Jesus. But he couldn't. Oh, he could pray for others—Mrs. G., Griff, his dad. Even strangers. But not himself.

Anger lay between him and Jesus like a desolate wasteland. No way around it, no way across it.

Abruptly he stood and walked away, leaving behind the chapel and the peace that God could offer.

He wound his way through the hospital to the cafeteria where he ordered two cups of coffee to go. Not knowing how Rachel took hers, he stuck packets of sugar and cream in his pocket. As the elevator doors opened and he stepped into the hall, he saw Rachel and Dr. Kessler talking outside Mrs. G.'s door.

Josh walked forward, sympathy stirring as he watched Rachel pace, her arms wrapping and unwrapping about her middle. Her normally creamy complexion had gone pasty white and the small splattering of freckles across the bridge of her nose stood out in stark contrast. The agitation so obvious in her posture belied her coldness, and Josh fought the urge to enfold her in his arms. He approached, stopping a few paces away.

"You can't rule out NDGA. There've been tremendous results with the use of chaparral tea in persons with cancerous tumors.''

''I'm not denying that, Dr. Maguire. But I don't believe it will help Olivia.''

Rachel stopped her pacing and glared at Dr. Kessler. ''But it could help. We have to at least try.''

''The best we can do for Olivia is make her comfortable.''

''The *best* we can do is make her better.''

''She's entered the last stages. Even the chemo's questionable at this point.''

Sharp, ugly pain gripped Rachel's insides. It was her mother's plight all over again. Everything they knew to do was being done, but they held little hope. Helplessness clawed its way to the surface. She wanted to cry, to find a dark place and curl into a tiny ball to escape this nightmare. She gritted her teeth and fought for composure. Mom G. needed her to be strong and she *would* be strong, because the alternative was breaking down in hysterics and that was unacceptable. There had to be hope. ''But you'll continue with the chemo?''

''For now.''

''Then the tea could make her more comfortable.''

A sad, patronizing smile touched Dr. Kessler's lips. Rachel wanted to scream. The man didn't get it. They couldn't just give up on Mom G.

''All right, Dr. Maguire. I'll see what we can do about getting some chaparral tea.''

The small victory did nothing to dispel the ache in Rachel's heart. Deep down, she knew he was agreeing for her sake, not Mom G.'s. But she didn't care if it meant Mom G. had a chance to live a little longer.

"Now, if you'll excuse me. I'll go check on Olivia." Dr. Kessler retreated into Mom G.'s room.

Rachel stared at the closed door, feeling as though her universe had been knocked off-kilter. She should be the one checking on the patient, the one in control. But here, in this hospital, she was a loved one, not a doctor.

"Rachel."

She braced herself and turned to find Josh's expressive hazel eyes regarding her with compassion. Her arms dropped to her sides and she resisted clenching her fists. She wouldn't let him see how scared and uncertain she felt. She didn't need his pity.

And his comfort would ultimately only harm her.

He held out a steaming cup of coffee and she relaxed slightly.

His square, blunt fingers engulfed the disposable cup and thin white scars stood out against his tanned skin. As she took the drink she noticed her own hand, the skin pale and smooth from years of being scrubbed and encased in rubber gloves. How different their lives had become.

The brush of his fingers scorched her skin. A splash of coffee wouldn't have been as hot. Or as painful. She steadied herself. "Thank you. That was very thoughtful."

Just as she feared, his presence *was* comforting. Like a solid oak tree in a windstorm. Able to sway and bend but never break.

"You're welcome." He stuck his hand into the pocket of his casual khaki slacks and pulled out packets of sugar and cream. "I didn't know…"

"Black," she said, moved by his concern.

Josh returned the items to his pocket.

Rachel took a fortifying swig from the cup and savored the robust flavor, until the hot liquid hit her empty stomach with an acidic thud. She grimaced. She'd forgotten to eat again.

"That bad, huh?" Josh asked, his expression softening as he gave a small laugh.

She sucked in a quick breath and could only stare. This man standing before her may be the boy she'd loved in high school but he'd matured into an appealing man she didn't know. A man who made her want to believe a dancing hot flame could heal as well as harm.

And she had no intention of playing with fire, no matter how fascinating the blaze.

The moment stretched to an almost unbearable ache, then abruptly Josh asked, "So, what's chaparral tea?"

Rachel blinked, but took her cue and slipped easily into her professional demeanor. "The tea leaves come from the creosote bush, which is found in the southwestern states. The healing properties of the tea have been used by Native Americans for centuries."

"And the ND…?"

"NDGA—nordihydroguaiaretic. It's the proponent in the plant that seems to help in reducing cancerous mass."

"You think this tea will help Mrs. G.?"

Her poise slipped a notch as she stared down at her coffee. She wanted to believe it would help, but the doctor in her knew the chances at this point were slim to none, just as Dr. Kessler had said. But she refused to give up and reject *anything* that might help. She hated this feeling of helplessness.

She shrugged. "At this point, it's hard to know what will help and what won't."

"That's a typical doctor answer," he said with the slightest trace of teasing in his tone.

She glanced up. "Pretty vague, huh?"

The corners of his generous mouth tipped upward and he sipped from his coffee.

"Habit, I suppose. As a doctor, you try not to give false hope or bad news before you're absolutely sure."

"Rules of the trade," he remarked dryly.

"I suppose."

They lapsed into silence again. Rachel drank from her cup and watched Josh. She tried to view him objectively. Adulthood had etched lines around his eyes, and the outdoors had weathered his skin to a burnished sheen. His broad shoulders looked as though they could carry heavy burdens. Sometimes she wished she had someone to share her load with, but her life didn't have room for sharing.

"So, Rachel—" Josh broke the silence "—I hear you recently got a promotion."

She met his gaze, expecting to be assaulted by the disdain she'd seen earlier, but his expression was curiously friendly, as if he'd just asked if she liked rainbows and sunshine instead of probing at an old wound. A wound inflicted by the choice she'd had to make.

Josh had offered her a different path, one so inviting that she'd begun to doubt God's plan for her life. But, no matter how tempting, it would have been selfish of her to choose Josh over what she knew to be her purpose. No matter how much it hurt.

Chapter Two

"Yes. Yes, I did," Rachel replied, proud that her voice didn't betray her feelings.

"Good for you."

Uncomfortable with the thought that he'd discussed her with Mom G., she wondered what else he knew about her. He certainly didn't know what was between her and God. No one knew how emotionally crippled she was because of the way her mother had died. If anyone found out then she would be perceived as weak. And if she were viewed as weak then she wouldn't be able to achieve her goal of making sure her mother hadn't died in vain. No one would take her seriously. "I've worked extremely hard to get where I am."

"The fast track to success," he stated, his voice devoid of inflection and his eyes now remote.

She narrowed her gaze. "I'm on the fast track. This recent promotion will be one of many. But it's not about success. It's about changing the way things are done so no one else needlessly dies. My ultimate goal is to be chief of staff in a prestigious hospital where I can further the research in new and innovative triage techniques.''

''That's certainly ambitious.''

''That's the only way things get done.''

He shrugged. ''Is being a doctor everything you thought it would be?''

Irritation flared at his casually asked question. She'd had to make a tough choice all those years ago. He'd forced her to make the choice. It was all or nothing with him. ''Yes, I love being a doctor.''

He nodded, but made no comment. He shouldn't be so calm and collected, not when her world was spinning out of her control. She wanted to shake a few leaves off his tree.

''It's who I am.'' She couldn't help the defensiveness in her voice.

A tawny brow arched. ''Must be very fulfilling.''

''What's that supposed to mean?''

Anger stirred in his eyes. ''Nothing.'' A leaf fell.

Something inside Rachel made her want to pick a fight. Anything to distract herself from what lay ahead with Mom G. ''You obviously meant something by that remark, Josh. If you've something to say to me, then say it.''

''You've changed,'' he stated matter-of-factly, his gaze assessing.

She almost smiled. Almost. The woman she'd become was very different from the young girl who'd left. ''What? I'm not mousy like you remember?''

''You were never mousy.''

She chose to ignore the compliment in his tone. ''My job's very satisfying. What's wrong with that?''

''Nothing.'' The tension visible in his jaw claimed

he was far from the ambivalence suggested in his tone. "But it doesn't leave much room for anything else, does it?"

"I've never wanted anything else." She narrowed her gaze. "Why are you still so angry?"

"I'm not angry." His denial rang false. Leaves fell all over the place.

"Yes, you are." She put voice to the suspicion she'd always had. "You're angry not because I became a doctor, but because you didn't get what you wanted."

He looked her square in the eye, his expression derisive and taut. "You're right, Rachel. I didn't get what I wanted. I wanted *you*."

"You didn't want me," she scoffed. "You wanted a *wife*."

"I wanted *you* to be my wife."

"No, Josh. You wanted a cookie-cutter wife. Someone you could put in a box and mold to your specifications. And it didn't take you six months after I left to find one, did it?" Her own anger and pain reared up, making her chest ache. "That only proves how deep your undying love went, doesn't it?"

He drew back. Hurt—desolate and unmistakable—darkened his hazel eyes. "I did love you, Rachel."

He sounded sincere. But then, he'd always sounded sincere. "Oh, save it, Josh. I'm not buying it this time."

"What did you expect? You left and made it very clear you weren't coming back." The sarcasm in his tone dug at her heart.

"But I hadn't given up hope that we'd work things out once I finished school." Hurt-filled tears burned behind her eyes, making her more angry that she was losing her control. Shaking her head, she admitted, "I lay in my dorm room every night and agonized over my decision. Was being a doctor worth the risk of losing you?" She gave a bitter laugh. "But I never really had you."

Josh opened his mouth, but no words came. His perplexed expression galvanized her into adding, "You never once checked on me. No phone call. No letters. Nothing."

He shook his head. "I was hurt and angry, Rachel. You chose your dream of being a doctor over my love. I certainly didn't think you wanted to hear from me." His tone seethed with anger and resignation.

"No, you were too busy planning your wedding." Thinking about the blonde who'd been after him all through high school made her insides twist with... jealousy? No, never. "And how's dear Andrea?"

A spasm of pain, or perhaps guilt, crossed his features. "Andrea's dead." He stepped around her and walked toward the elevators.

Shock doused her anger like a swollen rain cloud emptying itself. "Oh, no." Sympathy and regret tore through her, and she hurried after him. "Wait. I'm sorry. I didn't know."

He jabbed his finger on the elevator call button. "Not your problem."

She reached out, wishing she could retract her words. Josh reared away as if she were contaminated. Stung, she let her hand drop to her side. Feeling small and petty, she said softly, "I'm truly sorry."

The elevator doors opened and he stepped in. He turned and stared at her, his eyes cold with fury and his face a hard mask of stone. An oak tree never looked so intimidating.

"Josh, please," she implored, wanting somehow to make amends.

He looked away and the elevator doors slid shut in her face, leaving her alone.

Should she go after him?

Rachel took a deep, shuddering breath. Her unruly tongue had caused enough damage for one day. Leaving Josh alone and staying as far away from him as possible while she was in town was the best thing she could do for him...and herself.

Andrea was dead.

Compassion filled her heart to overwhelming proportions. She ached for what Josh had lost. His wife, his helpmate, his dream.

How long ago had Andrea died? How did she die? Did they have children? Goose bumps of remorse tightened Rachel's skin.

Years ago, she'd made it clear to Mom G. the subject of Josh and his bride was off-limits. She hadn't wanted her assumptions of his picture-perfect life confirmed. How arrogant she'd been.

The resentment she'd used to close off the pain of Josh's marriage deteriorated, exposing her to fresh wounds.

Slowly she walked back down the hall, rubbing away the goose bumps from her arm.

How had Josh taken the news of Andrea's death? Had he been with her at the end? Or had he been at work and received a call? How had the doctor told him? With compassion? Coldness? Understanding? Detachment?

The questions plagued her mind. And she welcomed them as she stopped in front of Mom G.'s door. As painful as it was, thinking about Josh kept her from worrying about Mom G.

Rachel leaned against the wall and closed her eyes. *Lord, why does life have to hurt so badly?*

She hoped, when all was said and done, she'd have enough mortar left in her to repair the crumbling wall around her heart.

"Dr. Maguire?"

Rachel's eyelids jerked open. She pushed away from the wall. "Dr. Kessler?"

He smiled kindly, his big gray eyes peering at her through his glasses. "Olivia's asking for you."

Relief surged in her chest. "How—how is she?"

"Holding her own for the moment."

Relief gave way to a dull ache at the words meant to give comfort but not false hope. She nodded her thanks and stepped into the room. Her footsteps faltered slightly as she approached the bed.

A nurse hovered over Mom G. For a panicked moment Rachel feared something was wrong, that she wouldn't have a chance to tell Mom G. how much she loved her, how much she appreciated her.

The nurse straightened and moved away, a reassuring smile on her face. Rachel resumed walking, her heart rate slowing to normal. As she reached the bedside, Mom G.'s eyes opened and she smiled. "I'm so happy to see you."

Rachel winced at how weak and breathless her mother sounded. Taking her hand, Rachel held on tight. "I'm sorry I wasn't here sooner." She wanted to say she should have been called right away but she didn't want to lay guilt on Mom G. It would serve no purpose.

"You're here, now. There's so much to say before—"

"Don't even go there," Rachel interjected. "We're going to make you well. I'm going to make you well."

Mom G. shook her head. "I'm dying, dear. We must accept that."

"Nooo!" Tears clogged her throat. She didn't like constantly being on the verge of tears. Even when she'd bounced from foster home to foster home, she'd never been this scared or so close to the breaking point. She wanted to draw into herself as she'd done as a child. But she couldn't. Mom G. needed her. And she needed Mom G.

"Rachel, please, don't cry. Let's use this time as best we can."

Rachel wiped at the tears unceremoniously slipping down her cheeks. She nodded. There was so much to say. "I love you. I want you to know how much you mean to me. I wouldn't be who I am today if you hadn't taken me in."

Mom G. squeezed her hand. "I hadn't ever planned on having kids, but when I was asked if I'd take on one child…I prayed and God urged me to say yes. I remember the first time I saw you. So skinny and scared. And you tried so hard not to show it. Now look at you. You're a grown woman and a wonderful doctor. Just like you'd planned. Are you happy, Rachel?"

Taken off guard by the question—surely Mom G. knew how much medicine meant to her—Rachel nodded. "Of course."

Mom G.'s eyes narrowed. "Really? For a long time I've had the sense that something's missing from your life. You've never talked about a man, or friends, even. Your phone conversations are always about your work. Work can't be the only thing in your life, Rachel.''

"It's not. I…'' But try as she may, she couldn't come up with an example. She worked six, sometimes seven days a week. Her apartment was small and cozy, but not a place she'd feel comfortable inviting anyone to visit. When she wasn't working she went to movies by herself or rented videos. She attended a Bible study through her church, but outside of class, she didn't socialize with any of the other participants.

When she wasn't knee-deep in research, sometimes she'd go to the library and read the latest medical journals and texts. Occasionally she'd dated. There'd been a fellow med student in school and a real nice guy from church a while ago, but over the years she hadn't met anyone she particularly wanted to pursue a relationship with. Besides, she didn't have time for men. Her life was the way she wanted it. No attachments. No hassles. No pain.

"Have you seen Josh?'' Mom G. asked.

"Yes.'' Remembering their meeting made her skin heat with embarrassment. She'd acted very badly, nothing like how she'd expected to act. Calm and cool, showing him that he couldn't affect her, which was how she'd dreamed their reunion would be. "He was here when I arrived.''

Mom G.'s expression became wistful. "It seems like only yesterday I was watching you go off to the prom with him. You two made such a handsome couple.''

A shiver of vivid recollection raced through Rachel. Her beautiful dress, Josh's tux. The excitement, the anguish. "I haven't thought about that night in years."

"The king and the queen of the ball," Mom G. teased lightly.

Rachel laughed, remembering the almost giddy feeling she'd had when they'd placed the gold crown on her head. "It was a perfect evening." At first.

"That was the night Josh proposed."

Rachel slid her gaze away from the intense look in Mom G.'s eyes. Her mind burned with the unwanted memories of that night. Josh had looked so handsome wearing that crown. They'd been dancing when he'd pulled her out onto the balcony and asked her to be his wife.

She'd been torn between her love for him and the path God had chosen for her. At the time she naively thought she could have both. She'd asked Josh for time, for him to be patient. Had expected they'd find a way to work it out that she could become a doctor and his wife.

But when it came down to accepting his proposal and his condition of staying in Sonora or the full scholarship to Northwestern, she'd chosen medicine because her soul would die if she didn't.

At that moment she'd known that God's plan for her didn't include the kind of love she'd have only with Josh.

"That was a long time ago and has no bearing on my life now."

Sadness filled Mom G. eyes. "I've respected your wish not to talk about him. But, dear, we need to have this talk."

"Why?"

"Because I love you both."

Rachel drew in a deep breath. She'd learned long ago it was better to meet a challenge head on rather than flee from it. "All right, if that's what you wish." She didn't want to have this conversation while standing. She sat down. "I know about Andrea."

Mom G.'s eyes widened. "Then you've talked with Josh."

"A little."

Mom G. shook her head; her wispy blond hair stuck to the pillow. "Such a waste."

"How—how did she…?" Rachel wanted to know, yet she knew sometimes there was protection in ignorance.

Mom G. pursed her lips. "An awful, awful car accident."

Rachel winced in sympathy. She shuddered slightly and suppressed the image of the last car accident victim she hadn't been able to save. "It must have been hard on Josh."

"Oh, honey, it was in so many ways." Mom G. stared into space for a heartbeat then turned to Rachel. "Do you have someone in your life?"

She blinked. "Uh…you mean a man?"

"Are you involved in a relationship?"

"No."

"I didn't think so. Good." Mom G. seemed to relax.

Rachel narrowed her eyes. "What do you mean 'good'?"

Mom G. gripped Rachel's hand tight. "Is your hope still in Jesus?"

Rachel gently patted the frail hand encased within her own. "Yes, my hope's in Jesus. He's my strength. You showed me that—you and Josh."

Mom G. nodded. "God loves you."

"I know. He's blessed me greatly. He brought me to you. Without Him and you in my life I'd...be lost. I'm doing what He wants with my life."

Mom G.'s brows drew together. "But He wants so much more for you."

More? She'd tried to have more once and she'd ended up with nothing but pain. Loving was a risk she was no longer willing to take. She shook her head. "I have everything I need. There couldn't possibly be more."

"What about love? Aren't you lonely?"

Mom G.'s words struck a cord within Rachel. She tugged at her bottom lip, loath to admit that there had been times over the years she'd watched couples, families, and felt an ache she couldn't explain. Was it loneliness?

Maybe.

But loneliness was a small price to pay to fulfill God's plan and to protect her heart.

"My life's very full. I might not have as many friends as I could…" Rachel frowned at the direction of her thoughts. Friends couldn't help in her quest to change emergency room procedures. "I just don't have time for relationships."

"Don't grow old alone. Believe me, it's not fun."

Guilt reached up and slapped Rachel. "I'm sorry I haven't been here for you."

Mom G. touched Rachel's cheek. "No, honey, you had to do what you needed to do. I regret that I never remarried after Frank died. I don't want you to make the same mistake."

Rachel nuzzled into the touch. She hadn't known Mr. Green. He'd been gone long before she'd come to live with Mom G. His picture graced the nightstand in Mom G.'s bedroom. "I'll be fine, I promise," Rachel assured her.

"Don't you think you'd be better with Josh in your life?"

Rachel schooled her features. She didn't want Mom G. to know how upsetting she found the subject of Josh. She didn't want her to know she still hurt deep inside her heart, in a far corner she pretended didn't exist.

"Don't avoid this Rachel."

Rachel met Mom G.'s gaze straight on. "There's nothing to avoid. Josh isn't a part of my life and he's not going to be."

Tears gathered at the corners of Mom G.'s eyes. "He needs you."

Mom G.'s sadness tore at Rachel. She wouldn't be able to make Mom G. happy. Not if her happiness involved Josh. "This is upsetting you."

"He needs you," Mom G. insisted.

Slowly Rachel shook her head. "He's never needed *me*."

"But he does. Rachel, he's always loved you and you still love him."

A double-edged sword of hurt and anger sliced through her. Her heart raced and her blood pounded in her ears. Josh didn't love her. She doubted he ever had.

As for her loving him… She closed her eyes briefly and hardened her heart. Been there, done that. Not doing it again. Emotions would not control her actions. Her goal in life was to make sure her mother hadn't died in vain, not to resurrect her relationship with Josh.

She opened her eyes and took a calming breath, regaining her composure. "It's not a matter of love. Josh had an idea of what he wanted in a wife and I wasn't it. He wanted someone I couldn't be."

"But that was then."

Rachel lifted one shoulder. "Nothing has changed. I'm still who I am."

"But they need you."

They? Rachel figured she must mean Josh and his father, Rod.

Mom G. dropped her gaze and sighed, but not before Rachel saw the disappointment in her eyes. She wouldn't say anything to encourage Mom G. She and Josh were history. And nothing could change that.

"Tell me about your new position."

Rachel nodded, thankful for a subject she'd have no trouble discussing, a subject that didn't make her suffer deep in her soul.

Because no matter how she looked at it, the subject of Josh would only bring her heartache.

The late-afternoon sun began to make its descent behind the mountain range, the fading light casting long shadows across the yard and backlighting Josh's Victorian house. Coming home at the end of the day always gave him a sense of satisfaction and peace. He'd worked long and hard refurbishing the broken-down Victorian, preserving as much of the original woodwork as possible. The overgrown land and swamp of a built-in pool had required hours of grueling labor to bring out the potential he'd known lay underneath. He'd created a stable sanctuary for his son and managed to ignore the vague feeling of incompleteness that plagued him at night.

Josh eased open the large solid-oak front door far enough to squeeze through. He didn't want a squeak of the hinge to herald his arrival. He wasn't ready to see his family, whom he could hear in the kitchen. He needed time, time to sort out the struggle going on inside of him.

He took the hardwood stairs slowly, placing each foot carefully in the spots where they wouldn't creak. In his room he closed the door and sat on the bed. With his elbows on his knees, he dropped his head into his hands.

All the way home he'd kept the thoughts at bay, forcing his mind into a blank numbness. But now they wouldn't be held back. Had Rachel really not known about Andrea? She'd seemed genuinely surprised, and remorseful. His heart told him she hadn't known, which only confirmed his belief that once she'd left town she'd never looked back.

Just like his mother.

Andrea. Sweet Andrea. Guilt engulfed him. He groaned, a deep, gut-wrenching sound that echoed in the quiet of his room.

Lord, it's too much to bear. Please take my guilt.

The plea went up as it had a hundred times before, but Josh snatched his plea back before he could feel any relief. He didn't deserve God's attention and mentally flogged himself with the pain of his guilt.

He hadn't loved Andrea enough. Not the way she'd needed to be loved. He'd tried to be a good husband. He'd encouraged her, supported her, provided for her. He'd given her everything he could but not the one thing she'd wanted—all of his heart.

Josh scrubbed at his face, trying to wipe away the sting of his self-loathing.

It was his *fault* Andrea was dead.

Because he couldn't erase Rachel from his heart.

Rachel. Was she right that he'd only wanted a wife, any wife? Had he been that arrogant and selfish? He'd tried to love Andrea with the same intensity he'd loved Rachel, but it had never happened.

Should he have pursued Rachel after she left? According to her, yes. But would his pursuit have changed anything? Would she have come back to the mountains to be his wife?

No, she wouldn't have.

And he couldn't have lived in the city playing second fiddle to her career.

Josh stood and paced, the leather soles of his shoes leaving indents in the dark green carpet. In the back of his mind a thought crept up, making him pause. Had he held his heart from Andrea because he was afraid to love her too deeply?

He clenched his jaw. It didn't matter now.

What he'd had to give hadn't been enough for Andrea. He'd lost her, just as he'd lost Rachel and his mother. Because he was not enough. And he was never going to make the mistake of trying to love again.

Now Rachel was back. He had every intention of not seeing her again before she left. He would have to plan his visits to Mrs. G. for when Rachel wouldn't be around.

Because this time he wouldn't be left behind with a broken heart.

Silvery light filtered into the hospital room, filling in the shadows created by the bedside lamp.

"In the emergency room we…" Rachel paused as

she noticed Mom G. fighting to keep her eyes open. "Here, now. I've talked enough. You should rest."

Mom G. smiled slightly. "Your life sounds very interesting, dear."

"It can be." Satisfaction in her career grew through the research she'd done and the triage techniques she'd implemented so far. But so much more could be done to improve the quality of patient care, and every day she spent in the emergency room was a new adventure.

She liked delivering babies the best. Liked the amazing miracle of life. God's wondrous process for continuing humanity. Sometimes she'd thought about switching gears and going into obstetrics or pediatrics, but she didn't want the emotional attachments those specialties would bring. In the E.R., patients came, they left. Her heart wasn't at risk and her mind stayed focused on her goal.

"Rachel, would you read to me for a bit?"

"Of course. What…?"

Mom G. pointed to the small bedside table. "My Bible's in the drawer."

She pulled out the black Bible, the same Bible that Mom G. had read to her from years ago. The worn black leather grew warm beneath her hands. "I remember this Bible." She glanced at Mom G. For a moment it appeared Mom G. had fallen asleep. Then she opened her eyes and smiled. Rachel looked questioningly at her.

Mom G. sighed. "I think the Psalms would be soothing."

Rachel opened the book and the once-familiar scent of Mom G.'s soft, powdery perfume wafted from the yellowed pages. A pang of nostalgia tugged at her heartstrings.

"Rachel?"

She paused and glanced up. "Yes?

"Would you do something for me?"

"Anything."

Mom G. gazed at her intently. "Would you call Josh?"

Rachel drew back. She didn't want to talk with Josh. "Call him?"

"I want to talk to you both."

"I'm sure he'll come tomorrow." Rachel would make sure she took the opportunity to speak with Dr. Kessler in his office while Josh visited so they wouldn't have to see each other.

Mom G. nodded. "Yes, but I want to make sure. I want to see you both together."

She lifted her brows. "Together?" Inside, she cringed. She'd come to town for Mom G., not to spend time with Josh.

"Please," Mom G. implored.

Rachel couldn't deny her the request. If Mom G. wanted to see them together then they'd be here together. Even if seeing Josh was painful, Rachel would do it, for Mom G. "I'll call him." So much for keeping her distance.

Mom G. relaxed. "Thank you."

Her chest hurt with love for Mom G. She leaned over and kissed her cheek. "You're welcome."

She sat back and stared at the open Bible in her lap. She didn't like the quiver of anticipation racing along her limbs at the thought of seeing Josh again. It was a purely physical reaction. Just because she found him attractive meant nothing.

She read King David's Psalms. *Lord, speak to me. I need Your guidance.* After all, she was who she was and the past was the past. There was only now, for Mom G. But Rachel didn't feel comforted by that thought.

A familiar sense of hurt filled her, reminding her of the pain loving Josh had caused. She would keep her focus on her path in life and fortify the fortress around her heart. She refused to allow him back in because once there he would make her want something she wasn't able to have—a life with him.

Chapter Three

Moonlight bathed the old Victorian in a soft glow as the community of Sonora settled down to enjoy another peaceful night nestled at the foot of the Sierra Nevadas. The Taylor men relaxed together in the cozy warmth of the living room. Josh had read in some parent-oriented magazine that children needed a calming home environment. He'd tried to make the inside of the house as comfortable and welcoming as possible with furniture that, in soothing greens and blues, invited relaxation yet was durable for a growing boy like Griff.

Josh liked this time of evening. He could talk to his son and find out about his day. What he'd done, seen, learned. And Josh would tell about his own day. Only, tonight he left out seeing Rachel. She wasn't a part of their lives and never would be.

Josh glanced at his watch. "Time for bed, kiddo."

"Aw, Dad. Come on. Just a little longer, please?"

Josh ruffled his son's hair. "Nope. It's time for bed."

"Will you read to me?" Griff asked as he slowly got off the couch.

He nodded. "Go get ready for bed, then pick out your book. I'll be up soon."

Griff walked to the bookcase where Rod Taylor stood with a book in hand. He kissed the older man's leathery cheek. "Good night, Grandpa."

Rod gave the boy a hug. "Night, pipsqueak."

Josh's heart swelled with love for his boy. Some said Griff looked like Josh. Josh didn't see it. His son had lighter hair, his eyes were more the color of moss than hazel and he had his mother's smile. Sadly Josh hadn't seen Andrea smile much toward the end. He should have tried harder to make her happy. A well-aimed stab of guilt twisted in his gut.

The phone rang.

Rod suggested, "Probably the station again. David Mackafee called earlier, wondering when you were coming back in."

Josh shrugged. He'd written out his schedule for the crew. Because of Mrs. G.'s illness, he'd been taking some personal leave from his duties as District Ranger for the Forestry Service of Tuolumne County. He would be going into the station in the morning, after he checked on Mrs. G.

He picked up the phone. "Hello?"

"Hello, Josh."

His brows rose in surprise to hear the female voice on the other end of the line. "Rachel?" His heart contracted painfully in his chest. There could only be one reason she would call him. "Is Mrs. G.....?"

"No, no," she said quickly. "She's holding her own."

The tightness in his chest eased. He glanced at his

father and son who both stared at him with anxious expressions. "Hold on," he told Rachel. "She's fine," he said to his family. Both Griff and Rod sagged in relief.

Then Rod arched a brow. "Rachel Maguire?"

"Who's that?" Griff questioned and moved to stand next to Josh, the top of his head reaching the middle of Josh's chest.

Josh shook his head and pointed upward.

Griff groaned and shuffled out of the room. As for his father, Josh said, "Do you mind?"

Rod grinned. "Not at all." And he sat back down in his recliner.

Josh rolled his eyes. Talking to Rachel on the phone while his father casually listened from his chair took him back to the past. But back then they'd had plenty to talk about—school, love, their future. The only thing they had in common now was Mrs. G.

"Sorry about that," he said into the receiver as he turned his back to his father.

"That's all right." Her voice sounded hesitant. "Mom G. would like to see you in the morning."

"I'd planned on coming by."

"But she wanted me to call and make sure. She…uh…hmmm…well, she wants to see us together."

Josh frowned. "Really?" He didn't want to see Rachel again.

"Yes. I don't know why, but I hope we can be civil to make her happy."

"I've never been uncivil to you, Rachel."

A moment of silence passed.

"Well, I mean, we could refrain from fighting. I—I want to apologize for earlier," she said in a rush.

The corner of his mouth lifted. At least one part of her hadn't changed. The old Rachel had always accepted responsibility for her actions.

"Forget it." He didn't need her apology. He thought about what she'd asked, then made a decision. "I'll be there tomorrow morning and I can be friendly for Mrs. G.'s sake."

"Excellent." She sounded pleased, but he couldn't be sure. "Goodbye, Josh."

"Bye." He slowly replaced the receiver. He hadn't wanted to see her, but he couldn't let Mrs. G. down. He'd tolerate Rachel if it killed him.

And when he thought about it, the best way to annihilate any feelings he harbored for Rachel was to be around the woman she'd become. She was so aloof and distant. Much different than she'd been in high school. Then she'd been open and friendly. Always looking for someone she could help. She'd needed to be of use.

Being a doctor must fulfill that need for her. But had becoming a doctor made her so cold? He supposed life in the big city could change a person, take warm people and turn them into an icy reflection of their former selves.

"You're going to be friendly with Rachel, huh?" Rod broke into his thoughts.

Josh shrugged. "Mrs. G. wants to see us both."

Rod looked pleased. "I might come with you."

"Fine." He didn't want to discuss Rachel with his dad. Didn't want to hear Rod's opinion that he shouldn't have let her slip out of his life. He'd had no choice. She was determined to go. "I'll see you in the morning." Josh turned to leave but stopped at Rod's soft chuckle. "What's so funny?"

"I have a pretty good idea what Olivia is up to."

"You want to let me in on the secret?"

Rod smacked his lips and grinned. "No. I'll let this one play itself out."

Josh frowned. His father and Mrs. G. were up to something. Rachel was the only girl Rod had ever approved of and Mrs. G., of course, loved her. But no amount of matchmaking was going to work. "You're a nut."

Rod wiggled his brows. "Takes one to know one."

Josh smiled. He loved his father and was thankful he'd agreed to live with him and Griff when they moved into this house. "Dad, what am I going to do with you?"

Rod laughed. "Hey, don't forget to call the station."

"Thanks."

"Sleep well, son. I have a feeling you'll need your strength tomorrow."

Josh shook his head in exasperation. He didn't relish disappointing Mrs. G. and his father, but nothing could bring him and Rachel back together. Their needs, their wants in life were too different. Rachel wanted success, prestige and a position of power. He wanted a stable, secure life with a woman who loved him enough to commit to him.

And Rachel wasn't that woman.

Rachel shielded her eyes against the sunlight streaming through the curtains of Mom G.'s hospital room. She blinked several times, trying to moisten her gritty eyes. She'd spent the night sitting beside Mom G.'s bed, too afraid to leave. She didn't want to get a middle-of-the-night call or find an empty bed in the morning. By staying, Rachel hoped she could keep death from claiming Mom G.

She listened to Mom G.'s labored breathing. Helplessness swamped her, making her head pound and her chest hurt. There had to be something more she could do.

She heard the door open. Expecting Josh, she fortified her nerves against his powerful presence and slowly turned around. The sight of a tall, older gentleman dressed in faded jeans and a dark patterned flannel shirt sent surprised pleasure coursing through her.

"Rod," she exclaimed softly. She glanced at Mom G., who still slept, then stood and went to the man who, for a time, had been the closest she'd ever come to having a father.

His infectious grin filled her with fondness. He hugged her for a long moment and she savored the steady comfort.

"Here, now." He drew back to look at her. "It's good to see you."

"And it's good to see you." She noticed his hair had turned a very distinguished gray and the crinkles around the corners of his hazel eyes had deepened. "How are you?"

"As ornery as ever."

"Some things never change," she teased.

He looked past her toward the bed. "How's she?"

"She had a rough night. The chemo took a lot of her strength."

He shook his head. "Such a shame."

"It is." Rachel knew Mom G. would be going on to a better place, but she didn't want her to go. She didn't want to think about the hole Mom G.'s death would leave in her life. Even though they'd been physically apart, Rachel took strength from both the knowledge that Mom G. loved her and from her weekly phone calls. Mom G. had always been there for her.

"Olivia's very proud of you, Rachel."

His words brought her pleasure. Mom G. had always encouraged and supported her goals. But the little girl she kept locked inside shook with dread. She was scared to be alone. "What am I going to do, Rod?"

He hugged her close again. "What are we all going to do? She's been a rock in all of our lives."

Rachel nodded, remembering how fond Mom G. was of Rod. Rachel had always wondered if their relationship went beyond friendship. Neither would admit—at least not to anyone else—to anything deeper nor act on it.

Speculatively she glanced at Rod. "You two are close, aren't you?"

His eyes twinkled despite an obvious sadness. "Yes, we are."

"How close?"

"Close enough." He winked.

"You…" A noise from the bed made her pause. Mom G.'s eyes were open.

"She's awake." Rachel breathed out a sigh of relief, thankful sleep hadn't turned into a coma. Each time Mom G. closed her eyes, the chance she wouldn't reopen them increased.

"She is indeed." Rod sat next to the bed and took Mom G.'s hand in his. "Olivia, my dear. I'm glad to see you. I came by early yesterday but you were sound asleep."

Mom G. smiled and her eyes glowed with affection. Rachel swallowed back the sadness that threatened to choke her. Mom G. and Rod obviously cared for one another, but now Mom G.'s illness was robbing them of their happiness.

"Time's…short," Mom G. said softly. "There's much to do."

Rod nodded. "Yes, Olivia. It'll all work out, don't you worry."

Rachel had no idea what they were talking about, and felt like an intruder.

"Rachel's…"

"Here," Rod interjected.

Mom G. shifted her gaze and Rachel stepped forward. "I'm right here."

"She's all grown up, Rod. All grown up."

Rachel savored the motherly words, tucking the tender feelings they evoked away in her heart for safe-keeping.

Rod grinned. "That she is, my dear. And a doctor, to boot."

The praise in Rod's voice pleased Rachel.

For a brief space of time, Rod and Mom G. silently communicated. Rachel watched, growing decidedly uncomfortable. The look in Rod's eyes as he gazed at Mom G. was more than affection.

He loved her.

A funny ache throbbed within Rachel's chest.

She refused to call it yearning.

But even if it was, she wasn't stepping off God's chosen path for her life. No matter what the cost to her heart.

Wanting to give Mom G. and Rod some privacy, and needing a moment to cool her thoughts, Rachel went to the window. The dew on the needles of the pines glinted in the sunshine like little teardrops.

"Rachel, would you mind getting me a cup of coffee?" Rod asked.

"Not at all." Rachel headed for the door, grateful for the task.

"Cream and sugar," Rod called after her.

She stopped at the nurses' station and smiled at the four nurses who bustled about. "Where could I get a cup of coffee?"

"I'll get you one," said a red-haired nurse who looked vaguely familiar.

"Do I know you?" Rachel tried to remember where she'd seen the striking woman.

The nurse smiled. "My name's Jamie. You were in my older brother's class. Bob Forbes."

"Okay, I remember him." She smiled back, remembering the red-haired boy who'd been the class clown.

"I'll be right back with your coffee, Rachel." Jamie walked away.

"Cream and sugar, too, please," Rachel called after the retreating nurse.

It was strange being in a place where people knew her. Not the doctor she'd become but the girl she'd been. That girl was gone, replaced by the professional woman who knew exactly what her life was meant to be. Giving hope and health to those who needed it. She never pretended to think she could save their minds or their souls. That wasn't her calling.

But their bodies she could fix by making sure the care in the E.R. was better so no one else would needlessly lose a mom. Yet a wave of helplessness swept through her. The one person most important to her needed her skills as a doctor and she didn't know how— She cut that thought off abruptly. She'd find a way to help Mom G. She had to.

Dr. Kessler came down the hall. "Dr. Maguire."

She tensed. "Doctor."

"I was hoping to see you before I made my rounds. We found some chaparral tea."

"Good." It may be a long shot but it was all she had.

"You realize the use of this tea is only effective when used regularly over a period of time."

She shot him a hard glare. She didn't need the reminder that time was an issue. "I'm well aware of the situation, Doctor."

She gritted her teeth against the gentle, pitying look in his eyes.

"Here you go." Jamie sailed up and handed her a disposable cup. Steam billowed from the milky, brown liquid.

"Thank you, Jamie. Doctor." She headed back to Mom G.'s room. She opened the door and slowly walked in, hovering just inside the room. Her throat tightened. Rod leaned in close to Mom G., still holding her hand. They talked in quiet tones. Rachel stepped back, intending to give them more time, but her elbow bumped the wall, making a dull thud. Rod glanced at her, and the corner of his mouth lifted before he turned back to Mom G.

Rachel continued forward. As she approached the bed, she heard Rod say, "I will do my best, my dear. I promise."

Mom G. nodded. "We have to try."

Rod stood. "Here's Rachel, back just in time. I have to take off, but I'll return this evening."

"Your coffee."

"Thank you." He took the cup and walked from the room.

"Such a nice man." Mom G. stared after him.

"He is." Rachel lifted a brow. "You and Rod have become close. You never said anything in your letters or phone calls."

Mom G. smiled slightly and a blush brightened her pale cheeks. Rachel laughed, loving the life shining from Mom G.'s eyes. If only she could hold on to that.

"Where's Josh?" Mom G. asked.

Rachel sat in the chair. "He said he'd be here."

Mom G. took her hand. "I'm going to rest until he arrives. Please wake me."

"Of course."

Mom G. closed her eyes. Rachel listened, thankful Mom G. breathed easier than she had earlier, but she couldn't shake the fear Mom G. might not reawaken.

Dropping her head onto the side of the bed, Rachel squeezed her eyes shut. *Lord, Your word says to count it all joy when we fall into various trials. This sickness is a trial that affects so many people. Mom G., Rod, Josh, me. Where's the joy, Lord? Show me, teach me. I don't understand.*

The low beeping of the machines, combined with Mom G.'s soft breathing, lulled Rachel's senses. Heart heavy with concern, she allowed herself to rest.

Josh pushed opened the door to Mrs. G.'s hospital room and stepped in. He stopped short when he saw Rachel sitting in the chair, her body bent forward and her head resting against the blue covers of the bed.

He could see the steady rise and fall of the blankets over Mrs. G.

They were both resting. He started to leave, but found himself staring into Rachel's crystal-blue gaze. She straightened and her black hair brushed loosely across her shoulders. She wore the clothes he'd seen her in yesterday. She hadn't left and he doubted she'd had more than a few moments of rest.

She blinked several times. "Hi," she said softly.

She sounded young and vulnerable, more like the girl he'd known. His heart twisted with longing. He pushed the unwanted emotion aside and told himself he felt sympathy for her for what was to come. Nothing else. "Where's my dad?"

"He left."

Josh frowned. "We came together, but he sent me to get coffee for him."

Rachel smiled ruefully. "With cream and sugar."

"Yes." He smiled and held out one of the cups in his hand. "I brought you one, too."

She stood and took the cup from him. Her hands shook slightly.

"Have you eaten?" He didn't appreciate the sudden need to take care of her.

"No." She sipped from the coffee cup.

He watched her press the cup to her mouth. He remembered kissing those lips so many years ago. Remembered her soft, pliant mouth beneath his, the way she'd felt in his arms.

Angry at the unwanted course of his thoughts, he averted his gaze. "You shouldn't drink that on an empty stomach. Why don't we go to the cafeteria and get some breakfast?"

She shook her head. "She wanted me to wake her when you got here."

Even though Mrs. G. lay a few feet away, being this close to –this intimate with—Rachel troubled him. It was too easy to remember the past, to remember how he'd once loved her, how she'd looked at him with love in her blue eyes. Too easy to remember that she'd wanted to be a doctor more than she'd wanted to be with him. And being a doctor had changed her. The woman standing before him set his nerves on edge.

"I'll let you do the honors." He took her cup and set it, along with his own, on the side table.

Rachel lay a hand on Mrs. G.'s shoulder. "Mom G., Josh is here."

Mrs. G. stirred. Her eyelids fluttered.

Josh's chest tightened. Mrs. G. had been such a godsend to him and his family. They'd kept in touch after Rachel left town, and when Andrea died, Mrs. G. had insisted on keeping Griff while Josh had dealt with the funeral arrangements. Then she'd insisted on continuing to care for his son while he worked. She'd become the grandmother that Griff needed.

And now they were losing her. Josh didn't know if his heart could take much more loss, and he worried what the loss would do to his son.

Mrs. G.'s eyes opened fully and she smiled weakly. "Thank you, Josh, for coming."

Josh moved closer. "Of course I'm here. I'll always be here," he said softly. From the corner of his eye he saw Rachel glance at him.

"We're both here, Mom G.," she said softly.

Mrs. G. lifted her hand from the bed and held it

out. Rachel immediately wrapped her own hand around Mrs. G.'s.

"Josh." Mrs. G.'s intent was clear. He hesitated before he slowly lifted his own hand and placed it over Rachel's. He kept his gaze trained on Mrs. G. and ignored the cool hand beneath his palm.

"I need a promise from…you both."

He glanced at Rachel. Her gaze met his. The wariness in her eyes reflected his own. Whatever Mrs. G. wanted, they would do everything in their power to make it happen.

As if she'd heard his thoughts, Rachel nodded imperceptibly and turned to Mrs. G. "Yes, of course, we'll promise you anything."

"Of course." Josh murmured his agreement.

His brows drew slightly together as he met the older woman's gaze. A mischievous glint twinkled in Mrs. G.'s eyes. Josh dismissed it as a trick of the light. Then she said, "Promise me that you two will take care of each other when I'm gone."

Josh stilled. Mischief nothing, the woman was bent on matchmaking! And he'd just given his word he'd do anything for her.

He hoped that wasn't a mistake he'd come to regret.

Chapter Four

Dismay sat heavy on Josh's chest, but he saw the fledgling hope in Mrs. G.'s expression and determination set in. He would do anything it took to fulfill her dying wish.

Hers would be one grave he wouldn't stand over with regret.

His gaze slid to Rachel. A slow red stain spread over her cheeks. She shook herself, glanced at him with wide, panicked eyes and then began to sputter, "Mom G. I…can't— You can't possibly expect…"

Josh tightened his fingers around Rachel's.

She ignored him. "We can't make a promise like that."

Josh applied more pressure. "Rachel, we can do this," he said with deliberate slowness.

Her head snapped toward him, her expression thunderous. "What?"

He was not going to argue with her in front of Mrs. G. It was bad enough that she was balking. He refused to subject Mrs. G. to the tempest that was about to explode. Because, like it or not, he was going to make sure she agreed. He couldn't let her live with the kind of regret that plagued him. He lifted Rachel's hand away from Mrs. G.'s. "We need to discuss this outside."

Rachel stared at him mutinously. "There's nothing to discuss. It can't be done. I live thousands of miles away, Josh."

He smiled tightly at Mrs. G. "We'll be right back." He tugged on Rachel's hand. She pulled against him but finally stood and jerked her hand from his grasp.

"Fine," she snapped, her expression softening as she looked at Mrs. G. "You'll be okay?"

Mrs. G. blinked. "Of course."

Rachel strode out of the room. Josh watched her go. She'd become quite a formidable woman. He normally chose to defuse confrontational situations long before they came to a head. That skill made him a good manager of the forestry team he was responsible for. But he found a part of himself looking forward to seeing the sparks fly, to being a part of the controlled energy that was Rachel.

Filled with anticipation, he winked at Mrs. G. before following in Rachel's wake, confident he could manage her.

Rachel's head was going to explode. Anger raged, pounding at her temples. She couldn't make such a promise. She wouldn't lie to Mom G. How dare Josh even consider promising something he had no intention of fulfilling?

She rubbed at her temples, trying for a calm that was proving elusive. She could control her emotions.

She was a doctor, a professional, standing in a hospital corridor, after all. She wouldn't cause a scene.

But the second Josh stepped into the hall radiating confidence, she whirled on him, her vow to remain calm pushed aside. "What was that all about? What are you trying to do?"

Rachel paced away from Josh in an effort to cool her temper.

Unruffled, he stated, "Trying to make Mrs. G. happy."

She screeched to a halt. "By lying to her? You think that's going to make her happy? Is your conscience out to lunch?"

Josh held up a hand. "Whoa, you need to calm down."

"Calm down?" She didn't appreciate him pointing out the obvious. Unfortunately her reserve of cool and collected was suddenly lacking. And it was Josh's fault. Something about the man he'd become caused her to lose her self-restraint. She didn't like being this out of sorts. It was too much; she felt too vulnerable.

She needed calm. She needed to breathe. *In slow, out slow, find the calm.* "We can't make that promise."

The dark green of his button-down shirt magnified the intent look in his eyes. "We said we'd do anything for her."

"But...not this. Are you out of your mind?"

"No." He shook his head. "I don't want to live regretting that I didn't do everything I could to make Mrs. G. happy."

His words struck her with sharp bites of guilt. "I want to make her happy, too, but I can't do this."

His expression hardened. "How difficult would it

be for you to set your feelings aside for a moment and do something for her?''

She drew back, stung. ''I'm not being selfish, Josh. I'm being realistic.''

His look said he didn't believe her.

''Think for a second, Josh.'' Her hand gesturing wildly. ''Your life's here. My life's in Chicago. And I'm leaving as soon as Mom—''

She froze. She widened her eyes and she covered her mouth with her hand as she realized what she'd almost said. A tremor assaulted her body. The reality of the situation hit her full force. No matter how good the medical care, Mom G. was going to die. Sooner rather than later.

Just like her mother had.

No! This was different. Her mother hadn't received the best care possible. Mistakes had been made, inadequate procedures followed. None of that was happening with Mom G. It was God's decision. *He* was in control.

She squeezed her eyes tight and fought the tears building, clogging her throat. She didn't want Josh to see her like this. She hated this feeling of utter helplessness.

God, I need you. I can't face this on my own.

She heard Josh let out an exasperated groan. Then his arms came around her, pulling her to his chest. She stiffened in shock. The odd combination of his woodsy-and-spice scent filled her head, evoking images of Christmastime. She longed to melt into his big broad chest and partake of the comfort being offered.

She didn't want his comfort. It hurt too much because it came from pity, not affection, but she couldn't deny the warmth soaking her through, making her conscious of every point of contact between them, every bunching muscle, every beat of his heart.

She swallowed her tears and broke away from him before she gave in to the attraction building between them.

Bereft of his warmth, she wrapped her arms around her middle. *Focus, Rachel, focus.* "What had Mom G. asked us to promise? To take care of each other. It wasn't like she was asking us to get married."

"Right." Josh's voice drew her attention.

She hadn't realized she'd spoken her thoughts out loud. "But how?"

"I don't know, but we'll figure out a way."

She stared down the hall. Maybe Josh had a point. It could be done. Through telephone calls, Christmas cards, e-mail. They could take care of each other long-distance. In ways that wouldn't wreak havoc on her life. Or his.

She straightened to her full height, still only barely reaching his shoulders. "You're right. We'll find a way. We can do this."

He smiled approvingly. "Yes, we can."

She resented how good his approval felt.

As Rachel swept by him and back into Mrs. G.'s room, Josh took a moment to recover from the shock of seeing Rachel almost shatter. It tore him up inside to know she hadn't completely accepted the eventuality of Mrs. G.'s death. Rachel was trying so hard to be strong. Behind her controlled exterior was a woman struggling against death and grief. He understood why Mrs. G. wanted his promise. When Mrs. G. died, Rachel was going to need an anchor to hold on to because the arctic storm brewing within her would be overwhelming. Whether he liked it or not, he would be there for Rachel because he'd promised.

Mom G. stared up at Rachel with anxious eyes. Taking her hand, Rachel sought to reassure her. "We promise to take care of each other." Rachel glanced at Josh next to her. His smile was pensive.

"Thank heaven." Mom G. relaxed into the pillow for a moment and then looked at them with worried eyes. "I need one more thing from you both."

Rachel braced herself. What more could she want from them? What more anguish would she have to suffer in Josh's presence?

Josh chuckled softly. "Whatever you need, Mrs. G."

"Rachel, you need to eat. You're too thin. Josh take her to get something to eat."

The motherly words touched Rachel deeply. "I'm okay, really."

"Please, Josh, make her go," Mom G. implored.

Rachel had had enough of Josh, thank you very much. "I'm not leaving you."

"I don't want you to get sick, honey."

A flutter of panic hit Rachel. What if she left and Mom G. died before she returned? Rachel knew she couldn't live with that. "Josh can bring something here."

"I want to sleep, Rachel. I'll rest better knowing you're letting Josh take care of you. As you promised."

Josh reached out and took her hand. She swallowed back the shiver of comfort in his heated touch. "Rachel, you need a break. We'll be back in an hour."

"Anything could happen in an hour," she whispered and pulled her hand free. Tears once again burned at the edges of her eyes.

"Do you trust God?"

She gazed into his warm hazel eyes. "Of course." Her answer was automatic. There was no question in her mind she trusted God. He'd seen her through so much and had given her the direction for her life.

Josh placed his hand on her shoulder; heat spread out from the point of contact. "Then let's entrust her to His care and ask for Him not to take her until you've returned."

This was a test of her faith and she hated the sudden hesitation gripping her soul. She wanted to know where Josh stood. Had his faith survived the death of his wife? "Is your faith that strong?"

Something akin to anguish flittered across his face, but then it was gone, replaced by determination. "Right now it is."

She had her answer. His relationship with Christ had suffered. She understood. To lose the one you loved so suddenly, without having a chance to say goodbye, would be enough to rock the most solid of foundations.

Mom G. squeezed her fingers. The weight of Josh's hand on her shoulder imprinted her skin. Her gaze darted between the two. Did she have enough faith? A still, quiet moment slipped by and Rachel was filled with a comforting peace. She nodded. *Please, God, let there be time for me to say goodbye.*

Rachel listened to Josh's words of prayer, felt them reverberate within her heart, filling her with comfort she gladly accepted. She'd always loved the sound of his resonant voice, could listen to him talk for hours. Time had only deepened the timbre, matured it in a way that was very appealing. And his words of faith were a balm to her weary soul.

"Thank you, Josh," Rachel murmured.

"Shall we?" He gestured toward the door.

Rachel kissed Mom G. goodbye, noting how drawn and exhausted she looked. Mom G. had expended a great deal of energy in securing the promise she wanted. It made Rachel more determined to comply.

Josh led the way out of the room. Rachel walked to the nurses' station, where she gave them her beeper number and elicited a promise from Jamie to make sure Mom G. received some tea before her next chemo session, which she was scheduled for within the hour.

"Everything okay?" Josh asked as they boarded the elevator.

"Yes." She followed him to the cafeteria.

Josh held open the door for her to pass through. The rattle of dishes and the rumble of voices greeted them. In one corner, a young mother spoon-fed a fussy toddler, while doctors and nurses, their white coats or green scrubs distinguishable, relaxed at several tables.

With metal trays in hand, Rachel and Josh went through the food line.

Even though it was only midmorning, Rachel chose a salad. She didn't want the heaviness of breakfast fare. Josh picked a hamburger and fries. "That food's going to sit in your stomach like a rock," she commented.

He grinned. "I'm a meat-and-potatoes kind of guy."

"Apparently."

At the cashier, Josh insisted on paying. Though she

was used to taking care of herself, Rachel didn't argue. She needed to think about something else. Anything. She searched her mind for a topic of conversation, but unfortunately with Josh, all they had was the past.

"Whatever happened to your '65 Chevy?" she asked as they took their seats at a table near the floor-to-ceiling window. The warm sun fell on her back and she shrugged out of her jacket.

"I still have her." Josh sat opposite her.

"She runs? You were always tinkering with the engine, replacing one thing or another."

The corner of Josh's mouth twitched. "Sort of."

"Do you ever drive her out to the lake?" Now why'd she go and ask that? Cherry Lake had been a special place for them. A place to go when the world was too hectic and intrusive. It occurred to her that there at the lake, alone with Josh, she'd never experienced that trapped, restless sensation. She mentally shrugged the notion off, attributing the lack of restlessness to being a teenager in love.

Any semblance of a smile vanished from his face. "No," came the terse answer.

Silence, dense and thick, filled the air between them.

Pushing her Cobb salad around with her fork, she searched for a neutral topic. "Does your dad still work for the forestry service?"

"He's semiretired." He picked up his hamburger and took a bite.

"That's nice for him."

"Uh-huh."

Frustrated that he wasn't being cooperative with

small talk, she watched him drown his French fries in ketchup. The red gooey mess didn't look healthy.

She ate slowly, her body recognizing the need for sustenance, but her mind rebelled, urging her back to Mom G. After a long moment of silence she tried again. "And you, Josh? What do you do?"

"I'm a ranger."

"You are?" Surprise echoed in her voice.

He glanced at her sharply. "I wouldn't lie."

"I didn't mean to suggest you would." She softened her voice. "You used to talk about going into the forestry service. I didn't think…" She trailed off, not wanting to offend him.

"You didn't think I would." He sounded amused.

"No, truth be told, I figured when you married Andrea you'd settle into a nine-to-five job and have a picture-perfect life." She'd imagined him living the fantasy. The fantasy they'd dreamed together those days long ago. An old Victorian house, the dog, the picket fence. Those were the things they'd wanted.

Only, as a doctor she didn't fit into his cookie-cutter world and she couldn't do what needed to be done from this hospital. The place where her mother had died.

Rachel noticed the ticking muscle along Josh's strong jaw. "I'm sorry. If you'd rather not talk about Andrea, I understand."

"Do you?"

The intensity in his voice made her wince. He was still grieving for his wife but she didn't know what to say or do to help him. The usual words of condolence she'd deliver to a family member of a patient didn't seem appropriate here. This was Josh.

"Dr. Maguire, Josh." Dr. Kessler approached the table.

"Doctor," Josh said.

Rachel rose, gripping the edge of the table, panic pounding in her veins. "Mom G.?"

Dr. Kessler held up a reassuring hand. "I'm on my way to see her. Just stopped in to grab a coffee."

She released her white-knuckled grip and sat down again. Josh reached across and took her hand, giving it a gentle squeeze. Comforted by his gesture, she gave him a grateful smile before slipping her hand away. His touch was too warm, too welcome. She couldn't allow herself the luxury of wanting his touch because wanting something she couldn't have was not her style.

"Dr. Maguire, our E.R. attending was very excited to learn you were here. I hope you'll take a moment and stop by the E.R. to introduce yourself."

Fat chance. She wasn't going anywhere near that E.R. Too many of her nightmares involved that place. Careful to keep her thoughts from showing, she smiled. "If I have time."

Behind his wire-rimmed glasses, Dr. Kessler's eyes showed disappointment. "I'll check on Olivia now."

Rachel watched the doctor leave. "What do you think of him?"

"He's a good doctor."

Josh's tone rang with certainty and she accepted his pronouncement.

She finished the last of her salad, then picked up her tray and stood. "I'm going back upstairs now."

Josh rose, taking her tray from her. "I've got it." He took their trays and deposited them in the dirty dish bin before coming back to stand beside her. "We could go down to the emergency room. We haven't been gone very long.''

Slipping her jacket back over her silk, short-sleeve top, Rachel shook her head. "I'm not here to work."

He arched a brow. "Too small-town for you?"

"No. I wouldn't be able to stay focused."

"Right. Focused."

The beeper attached to Rachel's waistband sent a shrill alarm ringing through the cafeteria. Her heart slammed against her chest. Mom G. Rachel couldn't make her feet move; panic gripped her, clogging her throat. Josh moved to her side, his big, warm hand cradling her elbow. "Josh, Mom G...."

"Let's go." The urgency in his tone clutched at her throat. She gratefully leaned on him as he propelled her out of the cafeteria and through the hospital.

Rachel and Josh stepped off the elevator and onto the fifth floor and sprinted down the corridor to Mom G.'s room. They skidded to a halt as a nurse emerged out the door.

"Is she...?" Rachel couldn't say the words.

The nurse smiled at her kindly. "She's waiting for you."

"Oh, thank you, God," Rachel breathed out. She swept past the nurse and into the room, aware that Josh followed closely behind.

Dr. Kessler stood at the foot of the bed, writing on the chart. He turned as Rachel approached. There was relief in his sympathetic eyes. "Her vitals are erratic. She's slipping away fast. It'll be only a matter of hours."

A heaviness settled on Rachel as she moved to the side of the bed and took Mom G.'s hand.

Mom G. stirred and opened her eyes. Her gaze focused on Rachel. "I love you."

Rachel swallowed the huge, burning lump in her throat and tried to smile, but could only manage a slight lifting of the corners of her mouth. Agony and grief gnarled in her heart. "I love *you*."

"You're my daughter. And I thank God every day that He brought you into my life." Her voice was weak, strained with the effort to talk.

Rachel let the tears slipping down her cheeks fall into her lap. She couldn't fight the pain of losing the only person who really cared about her.

"Rachel, happiness lies beyond what you think's possible. It's there waiting for you. You only have to have faith."

"I don't want you to leave me," Rachel whispered, shuddering with the intensity of her grief.

Mom G.'s grip tightened ever so slightly. "It's time for me to go be with my Savior. I've had a good life." She shifted her gaze away from Rachel. "Josh, you'll keep your promise?"

Josh's deep voice filled the room. "Yes, I promise."

Mom G. nodded and then seemed to shrink within herself.

Rachel pressed Mom G.'s hand to her cheek. Wanting to hang on, to somehow, with the force of her love, keep her from slipping away.

"I'll wait for you in heaven." Mom G. breathed the words with a smile and then her eyes closed.

Rachel refused to budge from Mom G.'s side. The hospital staff went about their business and Josh pulled up a chair beside her. Even though he didn't touch her, she felt his presence like a soft covering.

Two hours ticked by in agonizing slowness as Mom. G's breathing slowed to small hiccups of air.

Mom G.'s heartbeat fell, then stopped. Machines sounded a strident warning. Rachel instinctively reacted by rising, ready to begin resuscitation. She looked wildly at the others filing into the room. Everyone stood quietly by as Mom G.'s life ebbed away. "Why aren't you doing something?" she sobbed. "Let's bring her back!"

Dr. Kessler stepped forward and lay a gentle but firm hand on her arm. "She has a standing DNR. She was in great pain. She wanted to go."

Rachel looked down at her mother. *Peaceful* was the only word she could use to describe her. She was at peace with God.

Slowly Rachel sat back in the chair. A cold numbness seeped into her heart, spreading throughout her body. The two most important people in the world—her mother and Mom G.—had left her behind.

The weight of Josh's hand on her shoulder brought a fraction of solace to her restless thoughts. But that was an illusion, she reminded herself. A momentary respite from the grief welling up inside.

As soon as possible, she would return to her life and Josh would stay here.

Now she was truly alone on this earth.

Rachel sat near the window and surveyed the crowded church reception room. Among the various flower arrangements and tables filled with food, there were so many people. So many lives touched by Mom G. Some of the faces she recognized, others were new to her. Everyone had expressed his or her grief over

Mom G.'s passing and then wandered off to talk among themselves.

Her gaze dropped to the taupe carpet and the polite smile she'd worn all day faltered. She was out of place among these people. Without Mom G. she didn't belong.

A slight film of dust covered her black pumps. Though she'd numbly stood by the grave with eyes blurry from tears, the graveside service had been beautiful. Pastor Larkin had delivered a lovely eulogy and Josh had spoken, giving a sentimental testament to Mom G.'s memory.

He'd grown so close to Mom G. while Rachel had been so far away. She was glad the funeral was over. After the reception, she would meet with the lawyer, Mr. Finley, to discuss Mom G.'s estate and then she wouldn't have any reason to stay. She'd be free to return to the life she'd carved out for herself, the life God wanted for her. Strangely there was no peace in that thought.

Constrained laughter caught her attention and she looked up. Across the room Josh held a captivated audience as he talked.

She sighed. He looked handsome in his dark navy suit and tie, looking more like he belonged in a board-room than out fighting fires. He stood tall and carried himself with a confidence that she envied. He was a part of these people. He belonged here. She didn't.

A young boy moved to stand beside Josh. Shock momentarily wiped away the numb ambivalence that had taken ahold of her the moment Mom G. died. Rachel's heart pounded as she looked from the boy to Josh and back to the boy.

Even as Josh put his arm around the child and

hugged him, Rachel realized that this boy with his light-colored hair and expressive eyes could only be Josh's son. The "they" Mom G. had been talking about.

The child could have been *her* son.

She blinked and turned to stare out the window at the little town of Sonora. The quaint, turn-of-the-century homes, the cute little café that hadn't been there when she'd lived in the town and the gas station where Josh had worked during high school turned blurry through fresh tears.

Josh had a son. Why hadn't Josh mentioned him?

Why did she care?

She realized she didn't know that much about Josh and his life. She didn't want to know, she told herself. She couldn't change the past, could only accept it.

There was so much to accept.

The quicker she left Sonora and the memories behind, the easier the past would be to accept—and forget.

Chapter Five

Josh hugged his son close. He was grateful his father had had the foresight to take Griff to the hospital before school the day before Mrs. G. died. He hated to think of the pain Griff would have suffered had he not had the chance to say goodbye to the woman who had helped raise him.

Thankfully Rachel had been able to say goodbye, too. He scanned the crowd. He'd seen her earlier talking with Mr. and Mrs. Poe, then he'd lost sight of her.

She was putting on a good show of strength. Though her complexion was ghostly pale and her eyes were a little glazed, she'd smiled and moved gracefully through the funeral service and the reception.

She looked very mature and womanly in her black tailored suit with her hair pulled up into a fancy twist. When they'd talked briefly at the cemetery, she'd been distant and polite, but he could see by the tiny lines bracketing her mouth and the way she had to blink constantly to fight tears, that she was struggling to keep her composure.

Where was she? He frowned. She shouldn't have to deal with her grief alone. He started to usher his son toward the door in search of Rachel when he saw her sitting by the window. She looked composed and serene, but he knew inside she had to be crumbling. He steered Griff toward the window.

As they approached, she turned and he saw a flicker of an emotion he couldn't identify in her eyes. But then it was gone and she smiled with distant, polite interest.

"Rachel, I'd like you to meet my son, Griff. Griff, this is Rachel Maguire."

Rachel held out her hand. "It's nice to meet you, Griff."

Griff took her hand. "You're in the picture with my dad at Mrs. G.'s house."

Her eyes widened with surprise. "Yes, I am. How did you know?"

"Mrs. G. takes care of me when Dad and Grandpa work."

Rachel fought the burning behind her eyes at the boy's use of the present tense. She could only imagine the grief the child would suffer when he realized that Mom G. wasn't coming back.

Josh cleared his throat. She saw the same concern in his eyes.

"When you're ready to leave, let me know and we'll give you a ride to your hotel," he said.

"That won't be necessary." She didn't want to rely on anyone, especially Josh, for anything.

He gave her a pointed look. "Yes, it is."

Annoyance arced though her. Their promise to Mom G. didn't include his services as chauffeur.

He set his jaw and grated out a warning, "Rachel."

From across the room, Rod called out Josh's name.

Rachel turned her attention to Griff. "So who's your favorite baseball team?"

"The Mariners."

"Seattle fan, huh?" She nodded sagely. "I'm a Cubs fan myself."

"They're in Chicago."

Rachel laughed softly. "That's right, they are."

Josh placed a hand on Griff's shoulder. "Come on, Griff. Let's give Rachel some space. Let's go find Grandpa."

Griff gestured with his thumb. "He's over there."

"I know he's over there, son. I need you to come with me. We'll come back and take Rachel home when she's ready."

Rachel ground her teeth, but didn't say anything. She wouldn't argue with Josh in front of his son.

"Aw, Dad. I wanna stay here and talk to her."

"He can hang with me." Rachel blinked up at Josh, half expecting him to say no way.

"Okay. Then we'll take you home," he said firmly.

Their promise didn't give him a license to try to control her, but she didn't have the energy to point that out to him. "Fine."

Josh nodded and moved away, sapping the air of its heat and leaving her chilled.

"I have a baseball card collection."

Rachel turned her attention back to Griff. "You do?" An unfamiliar yearning crowded her senses. She supposed she was drawn to him because this boy was so like his father.

"It used to be Dad's, but he gave it to me. Now I collect them."

"How old are you, Griff?"

"I'm eight."

Rachel absorbed that information with a bit of shock. Josh and Andrea had waited before having a child. She'd expected them to start a family right away because that was what he'd wanted. "You look like your dad."

Griff grinned. "Everybody says that."

"I see your mother in you, too." His hair was more the color of Andrea's and the shape of his nose favored her, as well.

"You knew my mom?"

Rachel smiled compassionately. "We all went to high school together."

"What was she like?"

She blinked. "Don't you remember her?"

He shook his head. "She died in a car accident when I was a baby."

This news carried the weight of a punch to the solar plexus. Andrea had died nearly eight years ago. Rachel had assumed because Josh was still grieving that she'd died fairly recently.

Griff had grown up without a mother. Josh had raised his son from infancy all by himself. She had no doubts that Rod helped, but that Josh took on the responsibility made her admire him in a way she hadn't before. And made her ache for both Josh and his son. Ached for what they'd lost.

"Why are you crying?"

Rachel wiped at the tear coursing down her cheek and gave a shaky laugh. "I...don't know."

"Are you sad because Mrs. G. died?"

She nodded, surprised and relieved he understood that Mom G. was gone. She'd underestimated the child.

"She's in a better place now, where there's no pain."

"Did your daddy tell you that?"

"Yes. Mrs. G.'s in heaven with my mom."

Rachel hurt for this little boy, for what he'd miss. She hurt for herself, for the hole Mom G. left in her life. She hurt for Josh.

In an unfamiliar moment of need, Rachel hugged the boy. He smelled clean, like sunshine and fresh air. And when his little arms wrapped around her neck, she couldn't stop the sob that broke free.

"Shh, its okay," Griff said, his voice so grown up, so like Josh's.

Rachel forced herself to let go. "I'm sorry. That was inappropriate."

Griff cocked his head to one side. "Why?"

"You don't know me."

"Sure I do. You're Mrs. G.'s daughter. She talked about you all the time."

She swallowed past the lump in her throat. "Did she?"

"Yep. Hey, will you come to church tomorrow?"

That the next day would be Sunday hit her like a blast of cold air. Her normally ordered and scheduled life was in disarray. With all the emotional stress of the past few days, she'd lost track of time. Attending a church service would be soothing. Josh would be there, but she could handle that. "Yes, I will."

"Will you sit with us?"

Taken aback by the invitation, she struggled for an answer. "I don't know. We'll see."

"Aw, that usually means no. Please? You can sit next to me."

"Well…" She bit her lip. She didn't want to disappoint Griff, but…

"Griff, don't badger her." Josh's voice interrupted her thoughts and warmed her senses.

"He's not badgering me," she said.

"But he will until you say yes," he countered with an amused twinkle in his eyes.

"Aw, Dad."

Josh raised a brow and Griff rolled his eyes. Rachel smiled at the father-son exchange. Josh was a good father. His love for his son was evident in the way he looked at the boy, the way he displayed affection to Griff so freely. She'd always known Josh would be a good dad.

She sighed, feeling suddenly more alone and lonely than she'd felt in years. Josh had his son; she had no one. But she'd made her choice. A family wasn't part of her world, couldn't be a part of her world. Her job came first, would always come first. She doubted any man would accept that.

"You look tired," Josh said abruptly. "We should take you to the hotel."

Rachel stood. "You really don't have to do that. I'm sure Mr. Finley can take me there." She glanced around for the balding lawyer.

"No, we will," he stated. "Mr. Finley can stop by later after you've had a chance to rest."

She didn't like being told how she felt. "I'm not tired."

His expression became speculative and his tone softened. "Humor me, okay? Let us take you."

Griff slipped his hand into hers. "You can sit with me."

"Now how can you refuse an offer like that?" Josh asked.

She was sunk. How could she refuse Griff anything?

But Josh was another story. She couldn't decipher what she felt for him. The confusion left her wary and upset.

She wanted to go back to Chicago, far away from Josh and the jumbled mess of emotions he so easily stirred.

"Fine," she relented, only to have her nerves strung taut by the pleased look on Josh's face. Pleasing him shouldn't feel so good.

The tall, white-tipped, pointed steeple of the historic Red Church, its red paint gleaming in bright contrast to the clear blue sky, rose high above the maple and oak trees in the parklike setting of the church grounds. White-painted woodwork outlined beautifully etched stained-glass windows. The melodic strain of the church organ drifted out with the people as they exited through the open, wide double doors.

Rachel made her way toward the street, intent on walking back to her hotel without being waylaid by Josh.

The sound of pounding feet behind her drew her attention. She turned to see Griff skid to a halt before grabbing her hand. "Will you go get ice cream with us?"

Rachel laughed. "Don't you mean lunch?"

Griff shook his head. "Nope, ice cream."

His little face beamed and she felt tightness in her

chest she'd never experienced before. He looked so adorable in his navy slacks with a checkered button-down shirt coming untucked at the waist.

She glanced up as Josh approached. His tawny hair was combed back and the green stripe in his tie brought out the green in his eyes. A warm flush flowed over her skin. "Ice cream after church?" she asked.

He shrugged sheepishly. "It's tradition."

"Will you come? Will you, huh?" Griff tugged on her hand.

"I don't think so." The numbness she'd allowed to seep into her soul after Mom G.'s passing seemed to retreat every time this child was present, only to be replaced with a tender yearning.

The new feeling worried her; confusion was not something she allowed herself. She always knew exactly what she wanted and how to get it. Except when it came to Josh and now his son. She didn't like the out-of-her-control feelings spinning around her heart and mind.

"Please," he wheedled. "You can get any flavor you want. Right, Dad?"

"Sure she can." She heard the challenge in his tone.

Rachel tried to discern what was going on inside Josh's head. His expression gave nothing away. He looked decidedly…neutral, but his voice told her otherwise.

"I have things to do…." She stopped as Josh cocked one brow and Griff tightened his grip on her hand.

"You have all day to do stuff," Griff complained. "Please, please? I really want you to come with us."

Her mouth twisted in a half smile. She understood now what Josh had meant about being badgered. Ice cream did sound good, if only because it was a decadence she rarely indulged in. "Well…"

Griff pounced on her momentary indecision. "Yay!"

To Josh's amused expression, she said, "What? I like ice cream. Besides, he can be convincing."

"There's no doubt about that." Josh's mouth quirked up at the corners. His gaze narrowed slightly. "I went to the hotel this morning to pick you up."

"I told you not to," she countered.

He smiled with wry humor. "I went anyway."

She'd hoped he wouldn't. She didn't want him to think she'd deliberately stood him up. "I came early to spend a few moments of quiet before the service."

He nodded, but she could tell he wasn't truly convinced.

"Rachel?" a female voice called.

She turned to a see Jennifer Martin hurrying toward her. They'd been best friends in high school. Very different, not only in looks—Jennifer, blond and olive-skinned contrasted to Rachel's own dark hair and fair skin—but also in temperament. Jennifer was outgoing and confident. Rachel had envied that about her friend.

They'd spoken briefly at the funeral, but Rachel hadn't been in the mood to play catch-up on the locals. Jennifer had understood.

"Hi, Jennifer."

To Rachel's surprise, Jennifer hugged her again, as she had the day before at the graveside. Rachel wasn't accustomed to displays of affection from anyone other than Mom G. And Josh. Though she couldn't say that he'd held her at the hospital with any amount of affection, more like obligation. She stiffly hugged Jennifer back.

"We're going to get ice cream," Griff piped up.

Jennifer's speculative gaze traveled from Griff, to Josh and then settled on Rachel. "That's wonderful."

Rachel smiled tightly.

"I'm so glad to see you here," Jennifer said with a bright smile. "You'll have to come for dinner and spend time with my family. I can't wait for you to meet Paul and the kids."

"That would be nice," Rachel replied politely, feeling a pang of guilt. She wouldn't be in town long enough to make it to her friend's house, but now was not the time to say so.

"Good. Tonight then."

Before Rachel could protest, Jennifer turned to Josh. "You two come along."

"Sure, we'd love to," Josh replied.

"Great. It's settled then." Jennifer beamed. "Why don't you pick up Rachel and you can all come together?"

"We can do that."

"Hey, wait," Rachel interjected, hating the maddening way they were arranging her life. "I have things to do. I've got to organize Mom G.'s house, pack things up. I don't have time for dinner. I…" Her protest faded as disappointment clouded Jennifer's eyes.

Josh nudged her with his elbow and the look he gave her was a clear signal that she was blowing it and about to hurt Jennifer's feelings. "I suppose I can take care of everything tomorrow. Dinner would be great. Thank you."

The sparkle returned to Jennifer's eyes. "I'll see you all about five."

"Can we go now?" Griff asked, and gave Rachel's hand another tug.

Swallowing back the trepidation that she was getting in too deep, Rachel nodded and allowed Griff to pull her along.

The local ice-cream parlor was packed. The old-fashioned decor with its mahogany tables and soda fountain counter always gave Josh the impression of stepping back in time. He waved at several people and endured the assessing glances as he herded Griff and Rachel toward the back where he spotted a table being vacated by two teens. His gaze strayed over Rachel's long floral skirt, appreciating the curves and the way the hem flirted with her trim ankles.

"I want strawberry with caramel sauce on a waffle cone," Griff said as soon as his bottom hit the chair.

Josh raised a brow, not sure overloading his son on sugar was such a good idea.

"Awww." A fleeting expression of disappointment crossed Griff's face. "Okay, no sauce."

"What? No sauce? Outrageous." Rachel's light laughter captured Josh's gaze. She blinked up at him, her blue eyes full of merriment. "We gotta have caramel sauce on strawberry waffle cones."

"Yeah, that's right," Griff chimed in eagerly.

She raised her dark winged brows, daring Josh to say no. He didn't want to spoil the air of fun surrounding them. "All right, caramel sauce it is." So much for any semblance of nutrition.

Griff's exuberance exploded in a loud "Yeah!"

Rachel's pleased smile sent ripples of pleasure

down Josh's spine. Right now there wasn't anything remotely cold in her gaze. Her eyes were alive and warm, drawing him in, making him wish for the impossible, wish for a way to be enough for this woman. And wish the three of them could be a family. His stomach dropped. Abruptly he stood and headed to the counter. What was he doing having Rachel join them as if they *were* a family?

She's a friend, Josh admonished himself. Friends could have ice cream together. Friends could sit and have a decent conversation without their emotions being strung out to dry. Friends could laugh and enjoy each other's company without risking heartbreak.

His mouth twisted wryly. He was going to have to find a different category in which to place Rachel, because "friend" wasn't the correct one.

He paid and walked back to the table with three cones in hand.

At Rachel's appraising look he muttered, "It sounded good."

She laughed again. Josh liked her laugh. He'd forgotten how lyrical the sound could be, how her laugh wrapped around his senses. When they were in high school, Rachel's laugh was what had gained his attention.

As they ate their cones, Josh saw a side of Rachel he'd thought long gone. Here was the girl he'd been so crazy about in high school but there was so much more to her now. She'd seen things, experienced things that had changed her, given her depths that hadn't been there before.

Yet she was capable of an easy wit and gentle nature that made the time fly by. And Griff hung on every story coming from her lovely lips. How could his son help but fall for Rachel who at turns made Josh crazy with frustration and longing?

"Wow." Rachel sighed. "That was delicious. I haven't had ice cream in ages."

"Why not?" asked Griff.

"You know, I don't know."

She looked genuinely puzzled. Like the thought of enjoying something as simple as ice cream was foreign to her. What was her life like in the big city of Chicago? Did she have many friends? What did she do for fun? Was there a man in her life?

That last thought stopped him cold. He had no business even caring, let alone being tempted to ask if she had someone waiting for her return. Even so, curiosity about every facet of Rachel's life hounded him, made him want to know why the woman she'd become drew him to her despite his resistance.

They left the parlor and stepped into the sunshine. The parking lot hummed with the rumble of cars on the highway as well as the many entering and leaving the parking lot. The newly developed strip mall with the drugstore, bookstore, several specialty stores and two restaurants buzzed with activity as people meandered about, busy shopping and such on Sunday afternoon.

At the curb, Rachel touched his arm. "Thank you. I really enjoyed this morning."

He stared into those crystal-blue eyes and found he couldn't speak. The softness he saw spoke of caring and affection.

Her touch remained icy hot on his arm. An innocent touch that shouldn't cause such a riot inside.

He shouldn't let this get too personal, let the easy companionship of the morning cloud reality with wanting more from her. Yet he couldn't stop himself from covering her hand with his.

He told himself she needed comfort whether she wanted to admit to the need or not. She'd lost Mrs. G. The least he could do was offer some solace. Her eyes widened, and he was gratified to see a bit of the same chaos he felt reflected in her gaze.

She slipped her hand away. He wasn't surprised.

"We'll take you back to the hotel."

She drew herself up. The composed politeness he was beginning to detest settled over her lovely face and her petite form stiffened. Gone was the congenial woman of moments before. Now he was faced with the Rachel she'd become, the one he didn't understand or know how to deal with.

"That would be fine. I have things that need to be taken care of before we go to Jennifer's," she said stiffly.

And he would be there to help her take care of things, because of his promise, not because he wanted to. At least that's what he tried to convince himself of as he headed them out of the parking lot and drove them to the hotel.

When they arrived at the gray motel lodge consisting of ten single units, Rachel slid from the truck.

"Can I stay with you?" asked Griff, his little face full of eager anticipation.

Josh swallowed past the lump in his throat. His son's eagerness to be with Rachel was touching.

Rachel smiled, her blue eyes twinkling. "You're going to get sick of me if we spend too much time together."

"Naw, couldn't happen," Griff scoffed.

Josh ruffled Griff's hair. "We'll be seeing Rachel

tonight, buddy.'' He turned his attention to her. ''I'll be back in a while to help you with things.''

Her brows drew together. ''You don't need to.''

''But I will,'' he insisted.

''Josh, I'm going to rest for a while. Please don't come back until it's time to leave for Jennifer's.''

The edge to her tone conveyed the subtle message: *You're not wanted.* Well, too bad. She was stuck with him for the duration of her stay because that's what Mrs. G. wanted.

And he always honored his promises.

He chose to ignore the little voice in his head that wondered why it seemed like so much more. He didn't want more. Rachel would be leaving soon and he'd be safe to remember that spending time with her was for now only. There could never be a forever for them.

Chapter Six

Rachel was ready and fresh from a nap when the boys arrived to pick her up. She was thankful Josh had honored her wishes and not returned earlier. She'd needed the time to get herself refocused on her mission: See to Mom G.'s affairs and then head back to Chicago. She'd made an appointment with Mr. Finley to go over the terms of the will and sign the necessary papers.

The drive to Jennifer's went smoothly with Griff chattering away about an upcoming Boy Scout trip. The only trouble she had was keeping her pulse from racing every time she met Josh's gaze. He'd grown more handsome since morning. He wore dark denim jeans, a light blue chambray shirt with a white T-shirt peeking out at the V where the first three buttons were undone.

She forced herself to look straight ahead at the scenery going by as he drove, in an effort to keep herself from overheating. They turned onto a gravel driveway where Josh pulled the truck to a stop beside a white minivan.

The large, yellow with white trim A-frame stood on the top of a rise on the north side of the county. The wraparound porch cluttered with a smattering of toys added charm to the house. The laughter of children reached her ears and she couldn't tell if the sound came from inside the house or from the back where she'd glimpsed a lawn with a wooden swing set. On the evening breeze the scent of barbecue drifted past.

Griff bounded up the porch stairs while she and Josh followed at a more sedate pace.

"This is lovely," Rachel commented as they stopped in front of the large oak door. Sandwiched between Josh, his muscular body pressing into her as he reached to press the doorbell, and Griff, his small hand tucked tightly within her grip, she felt oddly out of place, yet not. It was a very strange feeling.

Heavy footfalls approached the door and it opened to reveal a man, average in height, with dark, short hair and a clean-shaven face. She kept her surprise in check. This man with his pressed khakis and white button-down shirt didn't match the type she'd always pictured with Jennifer. She'd figured Jennifer for the bohemian type of man willing to ramble around the world with his photojournalist wife.

The man smiled, his warm brown eyes crinkling at the corners. "Welcome. Hey, we're still on for bowling next Saturday?"

Josh flexed his fingers. "You bet. We'll whip up on Larry and Stan like last time."

"That we will." Paul ruffled Griff's hair. "Griff,

the kids are around somewhere. Why don't you go find them?''

Griff didn't needed to be asked twice. He disappeared from sight without a backward glance.

The man turned his attention to her. ''You must be Rachel.''

''Yes. And you must be Paul.''

''I am indeed. Please, come in.''

He stepped aside, allowing Josh and Rachel to enter. The comfortable coziness of the house surrounded her with peace. Even the clutter of toys couldn't diminish the rustic beauty of Jennifer's home.

The dining area directly across from the entryway held a large oval table set for dinner, surrounded by high-backed chairs and a high chair. In the living room to her right, Rachel noted the furniture was an eclectic mix of old and new. A huge stone fireplace dominated one wall.

''Jen's changing the baby. She'll be out in a sec.''

''Great.'' *Baby?* How many children did Jennifer have? Rachel tried to remember what Mom G. had said the last time she'd given her an update.

An enlarged photograph on the living room wall caught her attention. She moved to get a closer look. The peaceful serenity of the meadow scene struck a familiar chord. Bright yellow monkey flowers, indigenous in the Sierras, carpeted the sides of a meandering stream. The petals, which resembled the face of a grinning ape, were captured in vivid detail. Off in the distance mountains rose in majestic splendor meeting the sky in sharp lines.

''Jen took that.'' Pride rang in Paul's tone.

''That's why it looked familiar. Jennifer and I spent many summer hours in that meadow.'' She'd planned her life as a doctor and Jennifer had dreamed of photographing the world.

What happened to Jennifer's dream?

The sound of running footsteps echoed through the quiet of the house as Griff and three children of various ages and genders came skidding to a halt in the archway of the living room.

"Kids." Paul's deep voice brought the children to attention. "Meet Mom's friend Rachel. Introduce yourselves."

The tallest boy, close to Griff's age, smiled, showing even white teeth. "Hi, I'm Will."

Next to him a girl, younger and smaller, peered at her through a veil of blond hair. "I'm Krissy."

The youngest of the three, another girl with short, light brown curly hair blinked up at Rachel. "I'm Linnea. I'm four." She held up four fingers.

"Hello, Will, Krissy and Linnea. I'm pleased to meet you."

The three stared at her silently, assessing her. She smiled reassuringly, hoping she met with their approval.

"You're pretty," Linnea said, her little round face breaking into a grin.

Beside her Josh made a noise of agreement. When she met his gaze, his eyes were dancing with mirth.

Griff sidled up to her and took her hand.

"Okay, kids." Paul clapped his hands. "Go wash up for dinner. We eat in five."

The four kids turned and vanished down the hall just as Jennifer sailed in, carrying an infant on one hip.

"Hi. I'm so glad you could come." Jennifer gave

Rachel an one-armed hug. And then she gave Josh one.

"Me, too." She hoped her friend didn't hear her hesitancy. Though Rachel had worked with children often at the hospital, being in the midst of such a large brood was overwhelming. How did Jennifer juggle four kids?

"The barbecue's just about ready," Paul said. "It shouldn't be more than a few minutes."

"Need some help?" offered Josh.

"Yeah, come on back." Paul and Josh disappeared behind a swinging door.

"He cooks?" Rachel quipped.

"One of the perks of our marriage." Jennifer studied her with curious intensity. "Josh is a really good cook, too."

Hoping to distract Jennifer from the subject of Josh, Rachel held a hand out to the baby in Jennifer's arms. The little angel wrapped a chubby hand around one finger and pulled it toward his mouth. "Who's this?"

"Oh, honey, I'm sure Rachel doesn't want to become a pacifier." Jennifer extracted Rachel's finger from the child's grip. "This is Bobby. He's teething and everything goes in the mouth right now."

"Hey, Bobby." Rachel held out both hands. "May I?"

Surprise flickered in Jennifer's eyes. "Of course."

She passed the baby over and Rachel took him, loving the slight weight in her arms, enjoying the fresh, powdery scent coming from the baby's soft, downy hair.

"You're a natural," Jennifer declared.

Rachel laughed. "I'm a doctor. I get to do this occasionally."

"Dinner's served," Paul announced as he and Josh came through the swinging door carrying two large platters.

On cue the children raced down the hall and straight to their chairs. Griff took the empty seat next to Will. Rachel handed the baby back to Jennifer and then slowly moved to an empty chair. She sat with Jennifer on her right and Linnea on her left. Across from her sat Josh.

When Linnea's hand slipped into hers, Rachel blinked with surprise, but then she realized that Jennifer's hand was extended toward her. Around the table hands were held, forming a circle. Rachel took Jennifer's hand, completing the ring. As Paul said the blessing, Rachel felt a stab of longing for Josh. For the family with him that would never be. She forced herself not to open her eyes and look at him.

The meal progressed in a chaotic whirl. Rachel fielded questions about her life and in turn she asked about their lives. She found out Paul was a bank executive, Will liked basketball as did Griff, Krissy was passionate about horses and Linnea loved to have tea parties.

The children all had something to say, and the volume rose as they talked over each other. Jennifer fed the baby with intermittent comments and Paul listened attentively to each person while exchanging loving glances with his wife.

Rachel glanced at Josh occasionally and would catch him staring at her, heating her with the almost tender expression in his eyes. She smiled at him and felt like such a fake. She wasn't cut out for this kind of scene. Yet she couldn't deny the stirrings of need for such a life, for a family to call her own. She watched Jennifer. Her friend's eyes lit with joy and her smile came readily. Did she regret not pursuing her dreams? Could Rachel ever hope to have what her friend had?

Even if she could, that kind of life would never include Josh. His life was here; hers was in Chicago. A ribbon of sadness wound its way through her. She accepted it because she had no choice. She had to keep focused on God's plan for her.

After the table was cleared, Paul hefted Bobby into his arms. "Why doesn't Griff stay the night?" he asked Josh. "We have extra toothbrushes and he can sleep in a pair of Will's pj's."

"Can I, Dad? Can I?" Griff hopped in excitement.

"Sure, I suppose that would be okay since school's out now," Josh replied, earning himself a big hug from Griff.

"I'll get these rugrats settled in," Paul said as he ushered the kids down the hall.

Josh's gazed darted between the two women and then he called after Paul, "I'll help you."

"Chicken," Rachel teased.

He glanced over his shoulder. "I know to retreat when I'm outnumbered." He winked and then disappeared.

"Coffee or tea?" Jennifer asked once they were alone.

"Herbal tea would be nice."

Rachel followed Jennifer into the kitchen. The white-tile countertops, light oak cabinetry and blue-and-white gingham window coverings created an inviting and soothing atmosphere. Rachel dismally recalled her own kitchen with its harvest-gold counters, bare walls and dark cabinets.

She watched Jennifer go about the task of making tea, her movements fluid and natural.

"How are you really doing, Rachel?"

The intensity in Jennifer's voice grabbed Rachel's attention. Sliding onto a stool at the wide, white-tiled island in the center of the kitchen, she replied, "I'm hanging in there."

Jennifer's clear eyes searched Rachel's face. "I'm worried about you."

Rachel tilted her head, touched by her concern. "Why?"

Jennifer took the remaining stool. "Nothing specific. I just want you to be happy."

Rachel put her hand on her friend's hand. "Are *you* happy?"

Jennifer's smile brightened the room. "Yes."

"But you gave up your dream."

Confusion dampened Jennifer's smile. "What dream was that?"

"Traveling the world, taking pictures."

Jennifer laughed softly. "Dreams change."

Rachel sat back with a frown. "But you were so set on photojournalism."

Jennifer went to the stove. She was silent as she poured the tea. Carrying two mugs, she handed one to Rachel and then resumed her seat. "You know, I envied you so much when we were young. You always knew who you were and what you wanted out of life."

Rachel wrapped a hand around her mug. "So did you."

Jennifer shook her head. "I didn't have the conviction you did. It sounded good. Photojournalism." She gave a wry laugh. "That would've been a lonely life. I was afraid to tell you my real dream was to have a family.''

"Why?''

Jennifer shrugged. "Your dream was so lofty, so ambitious. I didn't want you to think less of me.''

Stung by that revelation, all Rachel could say was "Wow.''

Something deep inside Rachel shifted and an uncomfortable, wholly strange sensation filled her. For a pregnant, silent moment she stared at her friend, then comprehension dawned. She was envious. Envious of Jennifer's freedom to choose.

But Rachel had been given a choice once. Marry Josh or pursue medicine. She'd made the only choice she could.

A sharp pain banged behind Rachel's eyes. She pinched the bridge of her nose.

Her stirrings of longing for a family intensified, but along with that came the reality of what having a family for her would mean. The sacrifices and compromises that would need to be made. And the greatest sacrifice—the risk of loving and hurting.

Could she make those sacrifices, those compromises? And in doing so, would she be going against God's plan? How could she ever make that choice?

"Rachel, are you okay?''

"I'm getting a bad headache.'' She could hear the strain in her voice, feel the weight of her future crushing her heart.

Jennifer touched her arm. "I'm sorry if I upset you.''

With practiced effort, Rachel forced the pain to recede. "It's not you, Jennifer. It's everything. Losing Mom G., seeing Josh…'' The loneliness, the confusion. "Away from the hospital, I feel like I'm losing myself."

"Or finding yourself."

Jennifer's verbal arrow quivered in the center of the bull's-eye. "Maybe," Rachel scoffed lightly, trying to ignore the well-aimed words.

"I watched Josh tonight. He cares for you."

"Nothing could ever come of it. Josh and I both know that."

"We both know what?" Josh asked as he and Paul entered the kitchen.

Heat flushed her cheeks. "Nothing."

He arched a brow. "Looking pretty guilty for nothing."

Rachel threw a panicked glance to Jennifer, looking for help.

Jennifer flipped her curls and smiled serenely. "Coffee or tea, gentlemen?"

Rachel was thankful the conversation turned to world news events. She relaxed as the light banter among the four of them stayed on subjects that didn't include her and Josh in the same sentence.

She was painfully aware of Josh leaning against the counter beside her. His big hands toyed with a napkin, distracting her. He had nice strong hands. When he touched her hand, it seemed natural for her to curl her fingers around his.

"You tired?" he asked.

"Yeah, a little." She stared into his eyes. *He cares for you.* She was getting in way too deep. She slipped her hand away.

They said their goodbyes to Griff, who was snuggled in a sleeping bag on the floor of Will's room.

After promising Jennifer she'd see her again before leaving town, she followed Josh to the truck. He helped her in, his hand hot on her elbow, a shiver prickling her skin.

Alone with him in the truck, Rachel was acutely conscious of his masculine appeal. His muscled thighs and wide shoulders took up room, making her feel feminine in contrast. "It was a nice evening."

"You surprised?" He slanted her a quick glance.

She shrugged. "I didn't know what to expect."

Josh pushed a button on the dash and soft country music filled the cab. She couldn't tear her gaze from his profile. She liked the strength of his jaw and the line of his nose. Her gaze landed on his mouth, his lips. She clamped her jaw shut and turned away. She had no business fostering her attraction to him. No business wanting to kiss him.

They arrived at the hotel and Josh cut the engine. He shifted on the seat to face her, his arm stretching across the back of the seat, his big body leaning close. The tips of his fingers made little swirls on the top of her shoulder, setting off little sparks through her bloodstream. The light coming from the moon bathed his ruggedly handsome face in a soft glow, but couldn't disguise the magnetic pull of his eyes. She clenched her fist to keep from reaching for him.

"I have to go to the station tomorrow but I'll come back to help you at Mrs. G.'s as soon as I can."

"That's not necessary." It wasn't a good idea to keep seeing him when she knew it would only make leaving harder.

"I know it's not. But I want to." The husky timbre of his voice slid along her limbs like a smooth caress.

"What are we doing, Josh?" she asked, hoping to

bring some perspective into the intimate atmosphere surrounding them.

His fingers stopped. He drew back slightly. "I don't know. Taunting disaster?"

"I'd say so," she whispered, striving for calmness when her heart was beating wildly.

His mouth quirked up in a self-effacing way as he stared out the front window for a heartbeat. "I'll walk you to the door."

He climbed out and came around the truck to open her door. As she slid out, his arm encircled her waist, drawing her up against the length of his solid body. She tipped her head and the smoldering blaze she saw in his gaze ignited an answering flame inside.

She felt exposed, vulnerable to the attraction coursing through her. But it was so much more than purely physical and it scared her because any way she examined it, they had no future together. Giving in to this thing arcing between them would only spawn more regret and heartache. She deliberately shut down her feelings and pulled away from him.

On unsteady legs she moved up the stairs of her unit and unlocked and opened the door. She turned to say good-night, expecting he'd be where she'd left him by the truck, but found herself staring at his broad chest. She quickly stepped inside, keeping the threshold between them.

"It's best if you don't come tomorrow, Josh."

A look of implacable determination settled on his face. "Sleep well, Rachel. And I *will* see you tomorrow."

She watched him stride away and climb back into his truck.

"Sleep well?" she muttered as she closed the door

and listened to him drive away. He might as well have told her she could perform surgery with her arms tied behind her back.

Josh drove home on autopilot. He was all tied up inside. Hanging out at Jennifer and Paul's with Rachel at his side—as if they were a couple, a family—had felt right and natural. He'd liked it way too much. He'd let it go to his head. Let his guard down and had been tempted to act on the attraction building between him and Rachel.

She'd relaxed a bit tonight, as she had earlier at the ice cream parlor. When she wasn't all frosty and controlled, he really liked her.

But liking her and letting himself fall for her were two very different things. He was grateful she'd turned on the ice and reminded him how painful freezer burn could be. He'd be more careful in the future. He had a promise to fulfill, and as long as she was within his reach he'd do what he could to take care of her. But that's as far as he could let it go without costing him his heart.

Chapter Seven

Rachel wiped perspiration from her brow with the corner of her oversize T-shirt and surveyed the pile of boxes filling the back of Mom G.'s car. Driving again had felt strange after living in a city where she utilized public transportation every day. She made a mental note to contact Pastor Larkin and see if he knew of a family in need to whom she could donate Mom G.'s car.

"That should do it," she told the grocery clerk who'd come out to help.

"All right, you have a good day. And if you need any more boxes, you're welcome to come back and get them." The young man smiled and disappeared back into the grocery store.

She closed the back hatch and moved around Mom G.'s station wagon to the driver's side. Thankfully she'd left the windows down. The high sun raged like an inferno, letting everyone know that summer had officially arrived in the Sierras.

Driving along the pine-tree-lined streets, seeing the

houses of those she'd once called neighbors, Rachel shrugged off the feeling of isolation. This wasn't her life and this wasn't how she wanted to live. But as she pulled into the driveway of Mom G.'s ranch-style house, a wave of loneliness swept through her and she realized with a start that the sensation was all too familiar.

She felt the loneliness at night when she headed home from the hospital, she felt it on Sundays when she attended her church in Chicago and saw families sitting in the pews. She felt it every time she left Josh and Griff.

She was lonely. There, she'd admitted it. But she couldn't do anything about it. Not now, not until she returned to Chicago. Then she'd be able to formulate a plan on how to end her loneliness. Maybe a dog or cat would help.

After dragging the boxes into the stuffy, closed-up house, she faced the task of sorting through all of Mom G.'s items and packing what she wanted to ship to Chicago. The rest would be donated to Goodwill. Forcing her tears away, she walked through the house, and with each step, with every effort to keep grief from overtaking her, the numbness returned.

"Might as well start in the family room," she muttered, wanting to work up to the rooms that would be more emotionally difficult to face.

As she worked, her mind kept turning to Josh.

His steady strength appealed to her. Even when his overbearing behavior grated on her nerves, she found him compelling. Found comfort in his presence and in his sense of duty and honor. He was a man worth admiring. Worth loving. If only...

She ached for his loss, ached that he grieved for

the wife he'd obviously loved. Would Andrea always hold his heart? Or would he heal from her death someday and try to love again? What would it be like to be really loved by Josh, to have his stoic presence filling her life, balancing the irregularity of the E.R. with his unwavering strength?

Shaking her head at her own foolishness, she chided herself for thinking of Josh in terms of the future. His life was here—raising his son, working for the forestry service. Her life was across the country where her newest ideas in triage treatment were waiting to be implemented.

She reached for a platter from the cupboard and paused, remembering with vivid clarity the look in Josh's eyes the night before. He'd looked at her with such yearning and need. As if he wanted the relaxed and intimate atmosphere that had enveloped their time together to continue. As if somehow the past didn't matter, only the present. As if he could finally accept her for who she was. As if—

She slammed her thoughts down. Getting caught up in the moment was foolish. For both of them. Josh would never accept her for who she was. He would never accept that medicine was important to her and he would never leave Sonora. Allowing even a brief hope that somehow they could make a life together was beyond absurd.

She forced herself to concentrate on the job at hand. She moved with renewed purpose, her mind so focused that at first she thought a loud pounding on the door was merely an echo of the pounding in her head. She started out of her single-minded drive to get the job done. Hours had passed and dusk had fallen, creating shadows along the walls. She made her way through the house turning on lights as she went. She peered out the peephole and froze.

Josh.

If she didn't answer the door, would he go away?

The loud knocking persisted. No, he wouldn't. She took a deep, shaky breath, opened the door and drank in the sight of him in faded denim jeans and navy polo shirt that revealed muscled biceps. His hair looked slightly damp as if he'd recently showered, and the clean scent of soap and man filled her senses.

"You okay?" he asked, concern etched in the lines on his face.

Under his considerate regard, her heart raced and her body heated. With more effort than it should have taken, she composed herself. "I'm fine. Just working on getting things packed. What can I do for you?"

His brows shot up. "You could let me in."

"I don't think so. I asked you not to come."

"And I told you I would."

She couldn't argue that. She tried a different tactic. "I appreciate your trying to fulfill your promise to Mom G., but this is a little extreme. Honestly, Josh, the best thing you can do for me is leave."

He stepped closer, consuming the air, making breathing suddenly difficult. She involuntarily stepped back, trying to allow more oxygen to come between them. "Josh, please."

In a low, subdued voice he said, "Let me help. The quicker you're done, the quicker you can leave."

So that was it. Never mind that his words reflected her own thoughts. All his offers of help were to hurry her along her way. She shouldn't feel this bubble of disappointed hurt choking her. Shouldn't feel betrayed that he'd want her gone. She should be glad of the help, glad to move things along so she could leave and resume her life once again. A life without him.

The tumultuous conflict going on inside nearly made her stagger. But she drew herself up, arranging her features into what she hoped would appear as a polite, unaffected smile. "Of course. Leaving's my priority. But I don't need your help."

"I'd think that you'd want the packing done quickly," he grated out.

She bristled. "Am I not moving fast enough for you?"

"Frankly, no."

She couldn't let him in. She'd put off working on her old room and Mom G.'s room for fear of being swamped by her grief. *Lord, I need Your strength.* She was almost done with the rest of the house. "I can do this on my own."

He let out an exasperated breath. "Rachel, you shouldn't be doing this alone." His voice softened, wrapping her up in its even tones.

She resented how much she suddenly wanted him to help, wanted him to take her in his arms and make all the grief disappear. "I've done perfectly well alone for years. What makes you think I need you now?"

His quick intake of air was unmistakable. She peered up into his face, trying to discern his expression in the porch light. A shadow obscured his features, frustrating her attempt to decipher why her words would cause him distress.

"I can't believe you're going to renege on your promise so easily. Let me take care of you."

Stabbing guilt made her open the door wider and

step back. He stepped in, engulfing the house with his presence.

She hastily closed the door then moved to a stack of empty boxes and watched him survey the piles she'd scattered about the living room. "I've boxed up what I'm having shipped and the rest will be donated to Goodwill."

He nodded, his piercing, gold-specked gaze making a fire rise in her cheeks. She swallowed, fighting the attraction that always hovered close to the surface. He was a big, handsome man and it was natural for her to find him attractive.

Get a grip. She picked up a box and held it out to him. "We can finish the kitchen."

In two long strides, he came toward her and took the box. "After you."

She could do this. She marched past him and into the kitchen. They worked together in tense silence. Rachel found it hard to concentrate with only a few feet separating them. She'd catch herself watching his hands as they wrapped newspaper around dishes, those large masculine hands that with the slightest touch brought her comfort she'd never experienced with anyone else. She forced her mind to focus on her task. Soon the kitchen was packed.

"That's done." Josh stretched, his navy blue shirt pulling taut across his shoulders, emphasizing the broad width.

Rachel blinked and quickly turned away as she rose from her position on the floor where she'd finished taping closed the last box. Her stiff legs ached, reminding her she'd hadn't exercised in a while.

"Now where?"

Her stomach clenched in nervous agitation. "The bedrooms."

She hoped she could make it through this without breaking down. She didn't want Josh to witness any weakness.

Josh followed her down the hall to her old room. She pushed open the door, expecting Mom G. had already boxed most of her things and would have used the room for her own purposes, and was surprised to find it much as she'd left it. The frilly white bed coverings were neatly made, the shelves lining the walls held the various books and dolls she'd left behind.

Josh peered over her shoulder. "It's like walking back in time."

She closed her eyes against the sudden images of herself as a teenager. With graphic clarity, she saw herself sitting at the desk beneath the window doing her homework, her hair held high in a ponytail, her feet tucked beneath her.

She could still remember the night Mom G. had opened her door and said she had a visitor.

Josh had walked in with his easy grin and gentle manners. She'd secretly had a crush on him since the first day of high school. She hadn't known he'd noticed her. She hadn't known that one day he'd break her heart.

She opened her eyes and deliberately stepped forward and began pulling books and dolls from the shelves.

Without further comment, Josh dragged in several empty boxes and placed them at her feet.

"Thanks," she muttered, grateful for his thoughtfulness.

After a moment she paused and noticed his perplexed expression. The big, strapping male looked wholly out of place in the little girl's frilly room and clearly he didn't know what to touch and what not to.

Rachel stifled a smile. "You could strip the bed and pile it with the Goodwill items."

He flashed a relieved grin that hit Rachel with the shock force of a defibrillator. Quickly she turned back to her shelves. *Focus, focus,* she chanted inside her head.

After those first few awkward moments, they worked together like a tenured surgical team. She'd load a box, he'd tape it closed and fill out the address label.

Slowly conversation started, tentative at first. Rachel sought for neutral subjects and Josh seemed eager to keep their talk light.

As teens they'd had similar tastes in movies and books. Rachel was mildly surprised to discover that as adults they still shared many common interests.

They relaxed into a sort of rhythm, where one thread of conversation quickly led to another and another. They laughed and companionably argued over politics, choices for the Oscars and which authors should appear on the *New York Times* bestseller list.

In an amazingly short amount of time, they had her old room boxed up. "Thank you, Josh, for your help," Rachel said as they finished dragging the boxes into the living room.

"Sure thing." He held out his large hand. "Just one room left. You ready?"

She swallowed back the sudden tears that burned at the edges of her eyes. His offer of support nearly undid her. Clearly they both knew how hard this was going to be. She shored up her defenses. She couldn't show weakness, but she took his offered hand and allowed his warm palm to give her strength as they headed down the hall.

Mom G.'s room also was as she remembered. The double bed with its fluffy pink comforter, the dresser cluttered with trinkets and jewelry. The bedside table still held the picture of Mr. Green as a young man.

Rachel headed toward the closet, then stopped as she noticed the new pictures hanging on the wall. They took her breath away.

There were pictures of herself in beautiful frames. School pictures, pictures of her with Mom G., at the prom with Josh at her side, her graduation pictures from high school, college and medical school.

"She was very proud of you."

Josh's softly spoken words sent shivers of fire down her spine. If only he could be proud of her. She frowned at the thought and began pulling the pictures from the wall.

Lovingly she wrapped each frame in paper and stacked them in a box Josh had carried in. This time they worked in reverent silence, occasionally sharing memories of Mom G. Rachel kept more of the items from Mom G.'s room than she had from any other.

The large armoire that graced the wall next to the closet drew her attention. She'd find a place for it in her apartment. She ran her hand over the gleaming wood.

"When I first came to live with Mom G. I was a very scared little girl," she commented aloud. "Once again frightened by a new place, a new parent and a new set of rules to learn. One day I hid inside this chest.''

''What happened?'' Josh asked as he came to stand beside her, his presence comforting.

She smiled up at him, liking the way his interest was centered on her. ''Mom G. found me. Instead of the anger I had expected, she lovingly held me and told me stories until the fear went away. She was an awesome woman.''

Josh reached out and tucked a strand of hair behind her ear. His touch was electrifying as his knuckles grazed her cheek. ''She was.''

His gaze trapped hers. She was letting him get too close both physically and emotionally. She didn't want that, couldn't allow it. Only pain would result. She stepped back out of reach and gulped for air. ''I'll have the shipping company pack up the armoire.''

One corner of Josh's mouth tipped up as if he knew how he was affecting her. Disconcerted, she turned her focus to the closet. She touched each garment and Mom G.'s scent wafted up from the clothes, tugging at Rachel, making her ache.

''What's that?''

She wiped away a tear before facing Josh. ''What?''

He tilted his head upward. ''There.''

She followed his gaze. A white box on the top shelf of the closet bore her name. She glanced at him. ''Would you mind?''

Josh squeezed beside her, eating up space, and Rachel stepped back, nearly falling into the clothes piled on the floor. He reached out to steady her, his huge, strong hand closing around her forearm, sending hot sparks shooting up her arm.

"Thanks." She extracted herself from his grip and moved a safe distance way. Josh's proximity and his touch did funny things to her insides and she didn't want funny things going on inside. It made staying focused difficult.

He easily retrieved the box. "The living room?"

"Please." She headed down the hall. Josh set the box on the coffee table. She opened the lid and widened her eyes in pleasure. A tattered teddy bear lay on top of a scrapbook.

"Yours?"

"Yes." She picked up the bear and ran a hand over it. "My mother gave him to me before she died. I'd thought I'd lost him. Mom G. must have packed him up to preserve him." A lump rose in her throat. She held the bear close to ease the tightness in her chest.

Setting the bear aside, she picked up the scrapbook and laid it on the table. She sat on the sofa and flipped through the pages. Josh took the seat beside her, distracting her.

"Mrs. G. put effort into this," he remarked.

"It's wonderful." She couldn't believe how much she enjoyed looking at the pictures and the little anecdotes written beside the frames. The book chronicled her life with Mom G., starting with the first day she'd arrived to the last picture Rachel had sent. On the last line in the book Mom G. had written, "The rest of the book is for you to fill with pictures of your family."

Rachel stared at the words. Mom G. was her family. Without her, Rachel was alone.

As if he'd heard her thoughts, Josh asked softly, "Are those pages going to be filled, Rachel? Do you have someone waiting for you in Chicago?"

She slanted him a glance, aware of the anger stirring in her chest. Anger because he had no right to ask her that, anger because the answer was no.

"What do you think? No, wait." She held up a hand before he could respond. "What was it you said? 'No man would want to marry a woman whose priority in life was her career.' My priority is my career."

His words still haunted her. Every time a man had shown interest in her, she'd remember those words, remembered the pain of loving only to have to make a choice between the man and her God-given path. And her choice would always be the same.

Her life was about making a difference, about being a doctor.

"Rachel, I'm—"

"You're what? Sorry?" Rachel scoffed, her strength rapidly depleting. "Don't be. You were right. I wouldn't have accomplished what I have if I'd married or stayed in this town." She couldn't stand the pity in his eyes but hated even more that she'd validated his position on her career.

She closed the book.

Josh tipped the box forward. "There's something else in here."

She watched as he pulled a large manila envelope from the box and handed it to her. Anxious to get through this, she broke the seal and grabbed an official-looking file. Her name stared at her from the tab.

Ignoring the prickling awareness of Josh's gaze, she flipped open the file. The contents marked her progress through the Department of Child Services, starting with the day she became a ward of the state and continued on, noting every foster home with comments by the foster parents. She quickly read and absorbed the words. For out of the five homes she'd lived in, the comments were nearly the same: *"The child cooperates well, is very quiet and insecure."*

Rachel's mouth twisted. More like scared to death.

Mom G.'s name appeared as the last foster home. The remarks made by Mom G. touched Rachel deeply. To Mom G. she wasn't "the child," she was Rachel. A little girl who needed love and affection.

With a snap, she closed the file. She wasn't a little girl anymore, but a grown woman who just lost the last bit of family she'd ever known.

The hospital. The people there would be her family now. Her focus would be entirely on the patients, and their care, with no distractions.

Impatiently she dumped out the rest of the manila envelope. A hospital bracelet with her mother's name and the blue and white insignia of Sonora Community Hospital, a birth certificate and a small grouping of photos fell out.

Her breath caught in her throat. With shaky hands, she reached for the top snapshot. The woman in the picture had curly hair, which framed her face, and blue eyes sparkling with intelligence.

"Is this your mother?"

She nodded, afraid that if she spoke he'd hear her anguish. She had one picture of her mother that the social worker had given to her. It sat on her bedside table in a crystal frame.

"You look like her."

The compliment nearly shattered her composure.

Gathering every vestige of her control, she spread the rest of the photos out on the table. Five in all.

"I've never seen these. I wonder why Mom G. never gave them to me."

"Maybe she thought they'd make you sad."

In one frame, her mother stood on a beach staring out at the waves, her expression pensive. In another, her mother held a tiny baby wrapped in a pink blanket. The next was a park setting. A two-year-old Rachel sat on a swing, her mother behind her, joyous smiles on both of their faces. The last photo was of her mother, dressed up and looking like a princess.

"I wonder if my father took these?" Everything hurt inside and she willed the pain away.

Josh took her hand. His fingers wrapped around hers, anchoring her as the tide of grief began to rise within her.

"I don't even know who he was, Josh. What he'd been like. Why he'd left."

"I didn't know," he responded softly. "You'd said he was gone. I'd assumed he was dead."

"He was gone before I was born." She picked up the birth certificate. Her own. She pointed to the line where her father's name should have been. "'Unknown'?" Her voice rose, betraying the anguish building in her chest.

At sixteen she'd needed her birth certificate for her driver's license. Any hopes or plans she had of seeking her father out died when she'd seen that one word. "I can't accept he was some stranger my mother hadn't loved. Some one-night-stand type of deal."

"Maybe he hadn't known she was pregnant when they broke up."

Josh's compassionate reasoning left her with more questions. "Were they even married? Or just dating? Did they fight? Is that why she didn't want him to be a part of my life?'' She suppressed a shuddering breath. ''I'll never know. The answers died with her.''

Rachel's heart throbbed with longing. She had spent such a short part of her life with the woman in the photos. ''I don't even know what she was like. What had been her dreams, her struggles? There's no one for me to ask. She hadn't had any family that I could find.''

A tear slipped down her cheek and landed on the corner of one picture. The wetness distorted the film, like the tears in her eyes distorted her vision. Josh's arm came around her shoulders and a distressed moan escaped her lips.

Rachel didn't want him to witness her private breakdown. She didn't want to need his strength, his warmth. She tried to pull away but he wouldn't let go. His grip tightened and he eased her back against his solid chest. She resisted by leaning away from him.

''Rachel,'' he coaxed, his voice tender, caressing.

Everything inside screamed for her to protest, to run and seek solitude for her grief. She didn't need anyone. Yet his steadfast, comforting presence beckoned to her. She sniffed and shuddered as she tried to keep control of the tears.

When he turned her around, she dropped her gaze to the front of his shirt. She couldn't look into that handsome face and see the sympathy in his eyes. His hand reached out and gently lifted her chin. She almost died to see the tender caring in his hazel eyes. Everything inside melted liked chocolate over an open flame.

''It's okay to cry, Rachel.''

His compassionate words brought fresh tears. "No. I'm not crying," she sniffed.

"Stubborn woman," he muttered softly as he pulled her to him. "You have to let it out or it will eat away at you."

Rachel held herself stiff against his chest, but as his hand caressed her hair, and his heart beat a steady cadence against her cheek, her staid control slipped away. She wrapped her arms around him and a tremor worked its way through her body and a deep sob broke free.

She cried for the two mothers she'd lost.

As her sobs receded and the tears dried, she became acutely aware of Josh's arms holding her tight. The once-familiar pressure of his embrace made her snuggle closer. His woodsy, clean scent filled her senses. She clung to him.

She should let go. She should find her composure and graciously extract herself from his embrace. But she didn't want to, couldn't because of an inner need beyond her stalwart control.

Chapter Eight

Rachel eased back and looked up at him. He stared down at her with careful regard. How could he look at her with such tenderness when the heat in his eyes threatened to singe?

Her clinical mind registered that focusing on Josh kept her from dwelling on her mother's life so tragically cut short. Focusing on Josh kept the overwhelming grief of Mom G.'s death from engulfing her. Focusing on Josh made her heart pound and her limbs tingle with anticipation. Anticipation for what she didn't know. It went beyond the physical, to a heart-rending level. And it scared her.

She hated being scared.

In defense, her mind focused on the obvious—the awareness that overtook her every time he was near. As foolish as it was, she wanted to know what it would be like to kiss him as an adult, as a woman.

Before her brain could protest, she leaned forward and touched her lips to his.

An electric jolt sizzled between them.

Josh flinched.

Rachel tightened her hold around his waist and continued the kiss. Slowly, gently, he responded. His lips moved over hers with drugging intensity and she realized immediately she'd made a mistake.

Kissing him was far more potent than she'd imagined. She wouldn't just be burned, she'd turn to ash.

As Josh broke the kiss with a tortured sound, rejection settled at the bottom of Rachel's heart like a rock in a pool. Of course he didn't want her. He never really had.

She pulled away from him and took a deep breath, collecting herself. "I'm sorry. That was totally inappropriate."

His jaw clenched. "Why did you kiss me?"

"I—to distract myself from the pain," she admitted and wiped at her damp cheeks.

His guarded expression ripped at her insides.

She quickly gathered the photos and slid them back into the envelope.

A gigantic boulder lodged itself in the middle of Josh's chest as he watched Rachel. Taut lines of anxiety tightened around her mouth. Her struggle to maintain control was painful to watch. He hurt for her, could only imagine the depth of torment she carried. He'd never realized how devastating her mother's death had been to her. And to find out she didn't know her father's name—it blew his mind. His own mother had abandoned them, but at least at one time he had belonged to her. Rachel didn't even have that. His heart twisted with sympathy and a protectiveness surged through him. Mrs. G. had fulfilled the roles of both mother and father for Rachel, but now she was gone. It was up to him to be there for Rachel. If she'd let him.

She'd already expressed that she didn't want his comfort and he'd tried to give her space. But when she'd cried, his promise came slamming back to him. Mrs. G. had known what they'd find. That was why she'd insisted on their promise. He was honor-bound to offer his comfort and protection regardless of the cost to himself.

And cost him it did.

In the past few hours he'd glimpsed another facet of Rachel. She was a woman of strong opinions and tastes. Funny and charming when the wall of ice was down. So in need of care and compassion.

Then to hold her, to feel the luxury of her arms wrapped around his waist, had made his soul ache with longing for what might have been. For what would never be.

He sternly reminded himself that he wasn't enough for this woman. What he had to offer hadn't been enough twelve years ago and it wouldn't be enough now.

Her career was on the fast track. Onward and upward. She'd made it clear her life held no room for marriage, no room for commitment. Her career was her priority. That seemed such a joyless and lonely existence.

But when she'd kissed him and he'd felt the splendid caress of her lips against his own, he'd known that keeping his heart safe from Rachel while trying to be there for her was going to take every ounce of strength he could muster, and then some. He sorely wished he could find strength in God, but he'd lost the right to ask for God's help.

So instead he decided to take the high road. "It's late."

Rachel replaced the lid to the box. "Yes. It's been a long day."

Josh stood. "You should get some rest."

A little crease appeared between her blue eyes. A wry chuckle escaped. "I don't think I'll get much sleep tonight."

"Do you want to take the box back to the hotel with you?"

She chewed her bottom lip and stared at the box. Tears glistened in her eyes, making the blue brighter. She didn't answer. He couldn't stand to see her in such pain.

He reached for her, pulling her in again to the shelter of his arms. She wasn't nearly as resistant, and his blood surged at how right it felt to hold her close. "Leave the box. It'll be here tomorrow."

She nodded and allowed him to lead her to his truck. They drove to the hotel in silence. He felt protective of her and didn't like the idea of her alone with only her memories for company. "I'll stay. I can sleep on the floor."

Her gaze jumped to his. "No. That won't be necessary."

"Maybe not necessary, but the right thing to do." And the hardest thing.

She gave him a small, gentle smile. "I always liked that about you."

"What?"

She touched her hand to his jaw, the touch feather light yet searing. "Your sense of honor."

His chest swelled from her compliment. "I try."

She cleared her throat. "You should go home."

She was right, because staying might lead to some-place neither one wanted to go. "You sure you'll be okay?"

She shrugged. "It's better this way. I really did appreciate your help tonight. I'm glad you insisted."

"Just keeping my promise," he said evenly, but deep down a voice whispered it was so much more than that.

Her mouth twisted. "Well, it's still appreciated." She pushed open the door of her unit. "Good night."

He stepped back. "I'll have Dad check in on you tomorrow."

Rachel hated the little spurt of hurt his words caused. A foolish part of her wanted him to check on her. "Fine. Great."

He touched her cheek, the slight pressure like a brand against her skin. She swallowed and forced her-self not to lean into his touch.

"Call if you need anything."

She lifted her chin. "Of course."

His hand dropped away. "Good night, then."

And he walked away.

Rachel couldn't bear to watch his departure. She closed the door and slowly sank to her knees. She heard the roar of an engine turning over then the spray of gravel as he left the parking lot and drove away.

She hadn't felt this bereft since the day she'd learned he'd married Andrea. Mistakenly she'd thought focusing on her career had plugged the hole in her heart where her love for him had lived. But now she was left with a gaping abyss she didn't know how to heal.

And even if by some miracle she and Josh could find their way back to each other, she couldn't give up on the quest that had consumed her all her life, the task God had entrusted her with—to change the way things were done in the E.R. so that patients weren't needlessly lost.

And she couldn't do that in Sonora. She couldn't go into the E.R. where her mother had died. Not even God would ask that of her.

A line of Scripture came to mind and she clung to the promise in the simple words.

He heals the brokenhearted, binding up their wounds.

Peace and comfort would be hers, for God so promised. Her wounds would heal and she would return to her life, accepting the past and looking only to the future.

Without Josh.

The jingle of the phone roused Rachel from a fitful slumber. She opened eyes, gritty from crying herself to sleep, and glanced at the clock. Who would call at seven in the morning? Flipping to her back, she stared at the ceiling. Her body felt bruised, her eyes scratchy and she felt totally drained.

The phone jingled again. Rachel threw an irritated glance at the instrument sitting on the bedside table.

Even as depleted as her body and her emotions were, the steps of mourning that she'd gone through last night were necessary. She wasn't so presumptuous as to think she'd made it through the whole gamut of emotions that the grieving process produced, but her soul felt cleansed. She was ready to move on with her life. There were a few loose ends that needed her attention; then she could leave. Closure. Isn't that what they called it?

"You better not be bearing bad news," she muttered to the ringing phone, and picked up the receiver. "Hello."

"Is that you, Rachel?" a hesitant young boy's voice asked.

All irritation fled. "Yes. Griff, is that you?"

"It's me." His youthful exuberance returned full force into his voice. "Did I wake you?"

"Mmm-hmm," she answered on a yawn, and relaxed back on the pillow.

"Sorry, but I wanted to see if you'd go to Columbia with me today."

"Columbia?" The historic state park on the outskirts of Sonora was one of the finest restored mining towns in the county. She'd spent many weekends exploring the town. Once, in high school, her government class had held a mock trial in the old justice building. She'd been one of twelve students who sat in the old wooden chairs as jurors.

"Yeah, we could go gold-panning. Dad has to work and Grandpa doesn't want to go."

"Well…" she hedged. She'd love to spend time with Griff. She didn't have to be anywhere until later in the afternoon, when she signed the necessary paperwork to sell the house. She did have to call the shippers and Goodwill to arrange for the various boxes to be taken care of, but that wouldn't take long. And she loved to gold-pan. She and Josh had spent many hours at the task when they'd been younger.

"Will you go? Huh?" Griff's eager voice snagged her attention.

"Your dad's at work?"

"Yep, and summer vacation started yesterday.

Grandpa has business in town and he said we could pick you up then he'd drop us off in Columbia.''

It would be nice to see Rod again before she left. With Josh at work all day there wouldn't be any surprise meetings.

"I have to get up and dressed, then make a few phone calls."

"So you'll come with me?"

She laughed. "Yes. I'll go gold panning with you."

"Yahoo!"

Rachel held the phone away from her ear and grinned. Her mood lightened as energy seeped back into her body. Spending the day with Griff would make a good memory to take with her when she returned to Chicago.

"You sure you won't join us?"

"No, no. I gave up my gold-panning days long ago. But I sure appreciate you taking Griff. He's been wanting to do this for some time." Rod's gold-specked eyes sparkled with life. Even in his sixties he was a good-looking man with his thick graying hair and ready grin.

Rachel smiled. "It's really great to see you."

Rod reached out and patted her arm. "Now, don't you worry none. We'll spend some time together before you head back to your big-city life."

The way he said it, her life in Chicago sounded glamorous. Too bad there wasn't anyone there waiting to spend time with her. A familiar sense of loneliness gnawed at the edges of her mind.

A warm smile creased Rod's weathered face. No one smiled at her with real affection in the big city.

"I'll be back in time to get you to your appointment. Don't you worry about that," he said.

"I'm not." She turned to Griff. "All set to hit the gold?"

Griff scrambled out of the car in answer. He looked adorable in his loose, navy cotton athletic shorts and yellow-and-red striped shirt. By the size of his once-white sneakers, Rachel knew he'd grow tall like his father. Her heart pinched a little every time she looked at Griff. He resembled his father so much.

She turned back to Rod. "What will you do with yourself now?"

"I'm meeting with Pastor Larkin today about some renovations the church council wants done to the building."

"Tell him hello for me. And thanks for driving."

"No problem. You guys have fun and I'll see you in a few hours."

Rachel slid from the car and watched Rod drive away, his old white Buick ambling down the road. Tenderness filled her. For the first time she acknowledged to herself that she'd missed out by not having a father figure in her life. Rod was as close as she'd ever come and she loved him for that.

Griff danced from one foot to the other with anticipation, drawing her attention. "Let's go." His eyes widened and he pointed. "There's the stagecoach. Can we take a ride on that, too?"

The jangle of the harnesses on two big chestnut horses and the crunching of large wooden wheels over the loose dirt road heralded the coach's arrival.

Catching the boy's enthusiasm, she laughed. "We can do anything your little heart desires."

"Yahoo!" He tugged her along eagerly.

Rachel was glad she'd worn her running shoes. She'd forgotten that the streets were unpaved, and dust clung to her feet. And she had a feeling Griff intended to run her feet off. She couldn't think of a better exercise. The wooden sidewalks creaked as they stepped up onto the planks and headed to the stagecoach office.

Rachel paid for their tickets and they walked back outside to wait for the stage.

"I'm so excited," Griff whispered, loud enough that several people smiled.

In a stage whisper, Rachel replied, "Me, too."

The coach arrived and let off its passengers. Rachel and Griff climbed aboard. Griff scrambled to sit by the window and Rachel took the seat next to him. Soon the coach was filled and they were off. A speaker in the side of the rig showed the only sign of modernization.

The driver's voice filled the stage.

"Welcome to Columbia State Park. In 1850 gold was discovered and the mining town exploded with activity."

Rachel's mind wandered as she watched Griff, excitement danced in his eyes as he pointed out the window at various passing interests. She hadn't thought much about having kids of her own, not after Josh had married Andrea. Having a family had been relegated to "someday." "Someday" had always seemed far away, though looking at Griff she couldn't stop the maternal stirring in her spirit. She would have liked to have seen Griff as an infant, a toddler and a preschooler. To watch him discover the world and to teach him all the wonders of life.

A knot formed in her stomach. Could she be a good mom and still make a difference?

There were female doctors at the hospital who had families. They managed to be both. Though men dominated the upper management of the hospital, she would find one of her female peers and discover the secret to having a successful career and family. Finding a man to have a family with wouldn't be as easy. Especially not after seeing Josh, feeling his touch, his kiss—

Thankfully, the voice of the driver interrupted her thoughts.

"In the 1940s, the Parks and Recreation Department acquired the downtown district and restored it to its 1850-to-1870-era appearance. You'll find many of the shopkeepers dressed in nineteenth-century garb."

The coach came to a rambling halt.

"We hope you enjoyed your ride," the driver said. "Have a fun time in town."

Rachel and Griff disembarked.

A flash of awareness whispered down her spine like a warm breeze. Puzzled by the strange sensation, she glanced around then asked, "Where to now?"

"Gold-panning."

"Mind if I join you?"

Rachel started at the familiar voice and turned to find Josh leaning against a wooden railing that once had served as the hitching post for horses. Today he wore black shorts, showing off his strong muscular legs, and a red T-shirt emphasizing his broad chest. He looked virile and handsome, making her feel self-conscious in her khaki shorts and scoop-necked blue

T-shirt. She hadn't expected to see him and was shamefully pleased.

"Dad! 'Course we don't mind." Griff rubbed his hands together. "This is going to be so fun."

"I thought you were working today." Why did she sound so breathless?

He pushed away from the railing and strode toward her. A grin flashed, revealing his white teeth. "I decided to play hookey."

"What's hookey?" Griff asked.

Rachel met Josh's gaze and grinned, waiting to see how he'd explain that.

"Something we'll talk about when you're older."

"Aw, Dad. You always say that."

He gave her a pained look over Griff's head. She laughed, liking the shared moment.

"I thought we were gold-panning?" she said.

"Race you," shouted Griff as he tore down the road toward the end of town.

Josh let out a breath. "Sometimes being a parent keeps me on my toes."

"Blunder often, do you?" she teased.

"Only when I'm distracted by a pretty girl." He waggled his blond brows at her.

A blush crept into her cheeks. "Bad habit to have."

"Oh, I don't know." He put his arm around her shoulders and propelled her forward. "This is one habit I probably could get used to."

He was flirting with her and she liked it, even though it wasn't a good idea. He was still grieving and she lived thousands of miles away. She slanted him a glance and caught his gaze. The banked fire swirling in the depths of his eyes knocked the breath from her lungs. The day seemed suddenly ten degrees warmer as she felt an answering spark within her.

"Come on, you guys!" Griff yelled from the miner's shack front porch.

She blinked. A slow smile tipped one corner of Josh's mouth. He leaned close. She swallowed. Was he going to kiss her, here in front of everyone?

"Race ya," he whispered, and then started running.

"Hey," she shouted with a laugh as she made her legs go. They reached Griff at the same time, laughing and breathing hard. "I haven't felt like this in years."

Not since she'd left Josh behind.

His steady gaze bore into her in silent knowledge as if he'd heard her thought. She quickly glanced away, unwilling to confirm his suspicion.

Josh went inside and a few moments later returned with pans for each of them. They walked together to the small creek where the pleasant smell of pines mingled with the scent of wet earth.

For what seemed like hours they sifted through mud and dirt for any sparkling specks.

As they worked, Rachel enjoyed the natural way the three of them talked. She found out Griff dreamed to one day be a forest ranger like Josh and Rod. Griff's admiration for his father and grandfather was obvious.

Josh told stories about Rod and Mom. G. He spoke about his job and she could tell how much he liked the forestry service. She talked about being a doctor, but was careful to keep the focus light. She didn't want to ruin the easy camaraderie of the day with reminders of what her career meant to Josh.

At one point, she stopped to watch Josh help Griff with a big hard chunk of dirt. Their heads were bent together, their hands chipping away at the dirt. Would Josh ever remarry? She felt a little stab of jealousy for the woman who would capture his heart. She only hoped, for Griff's sake, Josh chose wisely.

"Well," Josh finally stood and stretched. "There's no getting rich quick for us." He glanced up at her. "Rachel, you okay?"

"Yes." She was determined to enjoy this time and not dwell on what couldn't be.

Griff stared at his empty pan with disappointment. "I thought for sure we would find some gold."

"How about finding some lunch?" Rachel suggested.

The pan forgotten, Griff's eyes lit up. "That sounds good. I'm starved."

"Me, too," Josh stated, his eyes trained on her.

She tugged on her bottom lip with her teeth and repressed a shiver as a charged current passed between them.

Feeling a little dazed, she followed the Taylors to a little deli that had been added to the storefront shops since the last time that Rachel had visited Columbia. They grabbed sandwiches and old-fashioned cream sodas.

When finished with their meal, they walked along the plank sidewalk, ducking into first a jewelry shop where they examined different sizes and shapes of gold nuggets. They continued on through town, looking at the antiques in one store, the tourist items in another. Then even went into the old jailhouse and marveled at the open jail cell with its thick black bars and single cot.

"This is what we need at home," Josh mused with

a teasing glint in his eyes. "A barred cell for when you misbehave."

"Dad," Griff squeaked.

A rhythmic pulse bounced off the stone walls. Josh pulled a tiny flip phone from his shorts pocket. After a brief conversation, he hung up. "I need to go to the station."

To hide her disappointment that the day was coming to an end, Rachel placed a hand on Griff's shoulder. "We'll be okay. Rod will be here shortly to pick us up."

"Right." His gazed searched her face. "This was fun, Rachel. I'm glad we were able to spend this time together."

"It *was* fun." More fun than she could remember having in years.

Josh hugged Griff and then sauntered away. Rachel stared after him, memorizing the way he walked, the way he carried himself. She didn't know when she'd see him again. And she didn't want to analyze how that made her feel.

"I know what we need," she said to Griff. "Candy."

His eyes grew wide. "That's right. We need candy."

The candy store was just as she remembered. Large glass cases filled to the brim with sweets. She recognized the sandy-blond-haired girl behind the counter as the younger sister of one of her old classmates. She surprised herself by asking, "Are you Kate?"

The girl cocked her head and squinted her brown eyes. "Do I know you?"

"I went to school with your brother Craig. My name's Rachel Maguire."

Recognition dawned in her eyes. "Hi, I remember you. You used to date Josh Taylor. Everyone was surprised when he married Andrea Marsh instead."

Rachel sucked in a breath. She placed her arm protectively around Griff's shoulders. "This is Josh and Andrea's son."

Kate smiled apologetically. "Oh, sorry."

Rachel wanted out of the store as quickly as possible. "We'd like some taffy, please." She hoped Griff hadn't caught the meaning of the exchange. She felt a tug on her hand. "Hmmm?"

"Chocolate?" Griff whispered.

"Some chocolate, too, please."

Taking their candy, they sat under a tree on a wooden bench. They sat in silence for a few minutes as they savored their stash. She realized with a start that she was content, relaxed. For the moment she felt comfortable in her own skin. The only thing missing was Josh.

"You were supposed to marry my dad?"

Rachel swallowed the suddenly sticky taffy. Tensing, she chose her words carefully. "At one time we thought we'd get married."

"Why didn't you?"

She tried to explain. "Sometimes we make choices in our lives that take people in opposite directions. I had to make one of those choices."

"Why?"

"Because ever since I was a very little girl I wanted to be a doctor, and the school I wanted to go to was far away. Your dad wanted to stay here." Rachel hoped that answer appeased Griff's curiosity and he'd let the matter drop.

Silence stretched out between them. Griff turned solemn eyes upon her and Rachel braced herself.

''Would you marry my dad now and be my mom?''

Chapter Nine

Rachel's heart threatened to splinter into a million pieces. He didn't understand the impact or the impossibility of his question. "Honey, I don't need to be your mother to love you."

"But being my mom would be better."

But if she gave up on what she was doing, more children might lose their mothers. Rachel sighed. "Your dad and I aren't getting married."

"How come?"

"We have very different lives. I live in Chicago where I'm a doctor and your dad has a very important job here. It just wouldn't work out."

"You could be a doctor here," he pointed out with a stubborn tilt of his chin. The gesture, so similar to his father's, caused a pang of tenderness to shoot through her.

Even if she could make the changes that needed to be made, while working from a smaller hospital, it wasn't possible for her at Sonora Community. Her mother had died there. She couldn't work there. Josh would never accept the importance of her career and she couldn't give up what God wanted her to do.

In a gesture that was becoming less awkward, she put her arms around Griff's thin shoulders. "I'm flattered you want me to be your mom. That makes me very happy."

He relaxed into her embrace for a moment before pulling away to stare up at her. His earnest expression was breaking her heart. "Do you love my dad?"

"I…" Rachel didn't have the words to explain her feelings for Josh.

She supposed she'd always love him with one tiny corner of her heart. The tiny corner that housed her girlish dreams. The tiny corner where there once was a wound so big she'd thought she'd never survive the pain. Today that part of her had seemed whole and complete. But that tiny corner didn't matter because in their situation, love wasn't enough. It never had been and nothing had changed.

Searching for words, she settled for a simple truth, even though she knew it was a cop-out. "God teaches us to love everyone."

Griff nodded thoughtfully. "That's true, because God's love and He loved us so much He sent His only Son to die for us so that we can go to heaven to be with Him."

Rachel smiled at Griff. "Did you learn that in Sunday School?"

"Yes and no. Dad taught me about God's love first, then I heard it in Sunday school."

"Your dad's a smart man." She was glad to see Josh had imparted to his son the wonder of God's love. She could still vividly remember the first time she'd heard the gospel message and the impact it had

had on her life once she really owned the promise in the words.

Mom G. had taken her to the Red Church right after she came to live in Sonora. The pastor had talked about Jesus and His death. She'd understood it, but hadn't really felt its connection to her.

Later, as she and Josh became close, he'd convinced her to join the youth group at church. There she began to comprehend the significance of God's mercy and grace and His redeeming love.

Glancing up from Griff, Rachel saw Rod walking toward them. "Here's your grandpa."

They stood and hurried to meet him.

"Hi. Did you have a good time?" Rod hugged his grandson and smiled over his head at Rachel.

"We sure did. Dad came to help, except we didn't find any gold," Griff told him.

If Rod was surprised that Josh had shown up, he didn't comment. Rachel suspected Rod had had a hand in Josh's appearance.

"Some days are like that. You'll find gold another time," Rod stated. "Right now, we'd better scoot or Rachel will be late."

Sitting inside Rod's car as it rambled away from Columbia, Rachel stared out the window. The smattering of huge white limestone boulders which miners, looking for gold, had once dredged out of the earth, stretched along the road between Sonora and the state park. Rachel knew that though the stones looked like a fun place to explore, the area was home to a large rattlesnake population. She'd found that out once the hard way.

Griff's continuous dialogue to Rod about their adventures drew Rachel's attention away from the countryside. As she listened to Griff recount the day, a stitch of sadness crept over her. It was the only time in her life she'd been a part of a child's adventures.

Rod pulled up in front of the brick law office of Mr. Finley. "We'll wait for you."

"You don't have to do that," Rachel replied as she climbed from the car, but secretly hoped they would wait. She really didn't want to be alone.

"Now, what kind of gentleman would I be if I didn't wait?" Rod grinned.

Rachel laughed with relief. "I shouldn't be too long." She hurried inside the old brick law firm.

For the sake of Griff and Rod, she blocked the swirling grief and sadness that hovered over her as she signed the necessary papers that established her as owner of Mom G.'s house and the papers that allowed the lawyer to act in her stead in the sale of the house.

She thanked Mr. Finley and quickly left. Sure enough, Rod and Griff were waiting. With a sense of homecoming that warmed and confused her, she climbed in the car and settled back against the seat. As Rod headed into the late afternoon downtown traffic, Rachel realized they were traveling in the opposite direction of her hotel. "Rod, where are we going?"

"I need to make a quick stop."

Rachel glanced at him sharply and caught the twinkle in his eye. What mischief was he up to?

He turned the car off the main street and onto a dirt road. Over a slight rise, a two-story Victorian house came into view. A large lush lawn stretched around the towering gray-and-white-trimmed house, an oak tree with a homemade wooden swing dangled from a low-hanging branch and cheery flowers grew in wooden flower beds along the porch. Everything looked well kept and cared for.

A black-and-white border collie came racing around the front of the old '65 Chevy pickup sitting off to the side of the driveway. Josh's house. The dog's welcoming barks and wagging tail told Rachel this was the family dog.

A flutter of nerves sent rippling waves across her skin.

"I just need to check something," Rod explained as he cut the engine and left the car.

"Want to see my garden?" Without waiting for an answer, Griff jumped from the car. With the dog barking a welcome at his heels, he disappeared behind the house.

Left alone, Rachel slowly emerged from the confines of the suddenly suffocating car. Her gaze took in the obvious love that had gone into the upkeep of the house and yard.

In the back of her mind a voice taunted her. *This is the house he'd shared with Andrea. The kind of house you could have had.*

Rachel pushed the thought away. She didn't regret the choice she'd made; she loved being a doctor. But a sudden desire for more crept in, making her wonder what their life would have been like had she chosen differently.

"Rachel!"

She followed the sound of Griff's call to the backyard, which proved to be as closely tended as the front. Griff waved from the middle of a large patch of freshly tilled earth and a few rows of green plants. She skirted around a built-in pool and across another nicely mowed expanse of lawn to stand beside the raised garden bed. "Wow, Griff. This is great." She breathed deeply of the sweet country air.

"This is my garden and I'm the farmer," he said proudly.

"Looks wonderful, Farmer Griff. What have you planted?"

She listened patiently as he explained about the types of vegetables he'd planted. He seemed quite versed in the care and feeding of his plants. Was that Josh's doing or Rod's?

After a while, Rod appeared from around the house. "We better get you home. It's almost supper time."

"Could Rachel have dinner with us?" Griff asked as he wiped his hands on his shorts, leaving stripes of smeared dirt.

"Sure she can. That's a great idea." Rod turned his gaze on her. "You don't want to eat alone when you could dine with us handsome men, now, do you?"

She laughed, charmed. "Thank you, but..."

He looked at her intently. "You already have plans?"

"No. I don't want to intrude. I'm sure Josh wouldn't want to come home to find company for dinner." The excuse sounded lame, especially after the day they'd shared, but she couldn't stay. She couldn't see Josh again. She wasn't ready for another ride on the emotional roller coaster that she rode every time he was near. "I really must leave." She headed toward the car.

"But Dad won't mind." Griff and Rod fell into

step with her. "He won't get home until late anyway."

Rod gave an assessing look. "We can take you home right after we eat."

"We can pick green beans from my garden. They taste so much better than the ones you get from the can," Griff added, his expression so earnest that Rachel stopped walking.

She bit her bottom lip. She didn't relish being alone any more than she had to. A problem she'd never experienced in Chicago. But she wasn't in Chicago, where her fast-paced world kept her from dwelling on things like loneliness and isolation. She decided to go with her current need. Besides, she wasn't ready for her time with Griff to end. She wanted to make the most of the memories.

"All right, let's go pick us some green beans."

Rod smiled with approval. She blushed and hurried after Griff, ignoring the certainty that leaving had just become that much harder.

Oh, Rachel. What are you doing?

The aroma of spaghetti sauce and warm bread greeted Josh when he walked through the front door. Laughter drifted in from the kitchen. Feminine laughter.

His brows snapped together. His father had left a message saying they needed Josh home right away.

As he made his way through the house, he could hear voices. His father's, Griff's and then a voice he'd thought he'd never hear in his home: Rachel's.

His father, it seemed, had taken up the matchmaking business where Mrs. G. had left off. But their efforts would never pay off, regardless of how easy and natural it felt to be in her company.

When his dad had told him that Griff and Rachel were at Columbia, all he could think about were the times they'd spent there years ago and how much he wanted to spend the day with Rachel and his son.

He'd wanted to make sure she was okay after the revelations of the day before; at least that's how he'd rationalized his need to be with them. It had been sweet torture. He hadn't wanted it to end. Reality really stank at times.

Rounding the corner to the kitchen, he stopped in the doorway. Griff stood on a chair in front of a large pot on the stove with a spoon in his hand. Rachel was leaning over his shoulder, his father's barbecue apron double-wrapped around her slim waist. One of Josh's old bandanas held back her ebony hair.

For a moment, dizziness swept through him. Seeing Rachel and Griff together, their heads bent close, made his heart ache. This was what he wanted. A wife to raise his son and a woman who would be passionate about their family, about him. A warm woman to love, who would want his love.

He gave himself a shake.

Rachel was not that person. Her career was her priority. She'd made that perfectly clear. She would never be content living here with them no matter how much fun they had together.

He exhaled slowly, finally remembering to breathe, and met his father's knowing gaze. Josh narrowed his eyes with silent reprimand. Rod shrugged, but his eyes held mirth and mischief.

"I didn't know we were having company tonight," Josh commented as he stepped fully into the room.

Rachel turned quickly toward him, her eyes wide. Obviously she wasn't a willing participant in his father's matchmaking scheme. Not that she'd ever agree to such a thing. She'd claimed she didn't need anyone and Josh pitied her for that. He'd have self-destructed long ago if not for his father, Griff and Mrs. G.

Sadness for Rachel, for the blows she'd sustained in the past few days and for her insistence of a solitary life, weighed heavily on his heart. She deserved his compassion and understanding. He'd made her laugh today. He'd do what he could to keep things light between them.

Griff waved the spoon, sending red sauce spraying everywhere. "Hi, Dad. What are you doing home so early? We didn't think you'd be home 'til late."

A splatter of sauce landed on Rachel's cheek but she didn't seem to notice. Her gaze pierced him. Her blue eyes darkened and her lips parted slightly. He recognized that look. The same one she'd had before she'd kissed him. It was a look that told him she saw him as a man in the here and now, not just as some guy from her past.

The uncomfortable pounding of his heart made thinking difficult. He broke the eye contact with Rachel and forced himself to answer his son. "I got a message—"

Rod cleared his throat, cutting him off. Josh shook his head at his father's antics. This had to stop. He and Rachel weren't going to get back together. The sooner his father accepted reality the better.

In a sudden flurry of activity, Rachel pulled off the apron, moved to the sink and washed her hands. "I think I should be leaving now. You gentlemen enjoy your dinner." She moved to the back door and then stopped. Slowly she turned around. "Uh, Rod, would you mind taking me back to the hotel?"

Eyebrows raised in innocent surprise, Rod asked, "Couldn't we wait until after we eat? I'm hungry." He deliberately moved to the table and sat down.

Her gaze darted between the men. She swallowed. "I don't want to intrude."

Josh moved to the sink and washed his hands. Her gaze remained on him and he sensed her reluctance. "I'll take you back after dinner, Rachel."

She pulled her lip between her teeth, looking a little forlorn and uncertain. Surprise flickered through him. Seeing the moment of vulnerability touched him, making him want to take her in his arms and hold her. If they could recapture a fraction of the comfortable and easy atmosphere they'd shared earlier in the day, then he could let her go.

"Stay and eat, please." He smiled reassuringly and stepped closer.

She stepped back, bumping into the door. She gazed up at him and blinked. Slowly, so to not send her running, he reached out and wiped the red smear of sauce from her cheek with his index finger. She swallowed. He held up his finger. "Sauce," he said, his voice low.

She nodded, her lips parted. Josh fought the urge to kiss her. To recapture the blissful torture she'd inflicted upon him the other day. Abruptly he stepped back. Kissing her in front of his son and father was not a good idea. In fact, kissing her at all was a very bad idea. It would only heighten his attraction to her and complicate an already complicated situation.

He held out a chair at the table. "Sit, Rachel."

A mutinous expression came over her lovely face.

"You sit." A spark of spunk flashed in her bright blue gaze.

"Are you going to serve us?" he teased, and liked the way she flushed in response.

She squared her shoulders and drew herself up, once again appearing cool and aloof. "No, I'm not going to serve you. You can set the table and get some serving dishes." Her tone softened as she looked at Griff. "You can come down from there and join your grandfather at the table." She threw Rod a murderous look before moving to the stove.

Josh hid his amused smile. She was something special. Running cold yet she could send his blood pressure skyrocketing with one smoldering glance. He staunchly forced himself to squelch the fierce need welling inside. He had no business allowing his feelings to run amok. She would be leaving soon, and he was not going to pine away for her a second time in his life.

He set the table and then tried to help her transfer the food onto the dishes, but she batted him away. "Utensils?" she asked.

"Yes, ma'am." He gave her a mock salute. She rolled her eyes but a smile played at the corners of her mouth, softening her features, reminding him of their day together. He'd liked the way they'd teased and flirted, like the way being with her had felt so right.

When all was ready, they sat. Josh took Griff's hand and then held out his other hand to Rachel.

She blinked.

Josh raised a brow. "For grace."

"Oh," she murmured before slipping her hand into his.

"Dad, would you do the honors?"

His father said the blessing over their food and thanked God for His abundance. In unison they agreed, "Amen."

Rachel gently tugged her hand from Josh's grip. He missed the contact and called himself a fool for wanting more.

Silence filled the kitchen as all four went about the business of eating.

"Yum," said Griff around a mouthful of spaghetti.

"This is delicious," agreed Rod.

"Wonderful," Josh added with approval.

Rachel blushed becomingly. "Thank you."

Josh couldn't take his eyes off her. Sitting with Rachel in his kitchen, at his table, as if they were a family, squeezed his chest. A shiver tripped down his spine, reminding him that letting down his guard, letting their relationship become something personal and intimate, was dangerous.

This woman had broken his heart once. He didn't want the past to repeat itself. He didn't want to be faced with not being enough.

His gaze swung from his son to Rachel and back. The look of adoration in Griff's eyes hit Josh in the gut. He had to protect his son from a broken heart. Rachel was good at breaking hearts. He cleared his throat. He decided to get things out in the open. Leave no illusions for Griff or himself. "When are you leaving, Rachel?"

She stilled. "After dinner."

He shook his head. "I mean leaving town. Going back to Chicago."

"Oh." She picked up her glass and sipped the water, her gaze chilly over the rim. "In a day or two. I have a shipping company coming tomorrow and Goodwill's also sending out a truck, but they weren't sure of the time. Why?''

''Just curious.''

Her look said she didn't believe him, but he didn't elaborate. Two days. Two days and then she'd go back to her life, leaving him behind again. Only this time he wouldn't ache and hurt like he had the first time. This time he wouldn't allow himself to feel the emptiness that had engulfed him years ago. And bigger mountains had been moved before.

Griff stabbed a forkful of green beans and waved them toward Josh.

He raised a brow. ''Yes?''

''Rachel and I picked these out of the garden.''

At the tender smile she gave Griff, a shaft of envy shot through Josh, surprising him with its intensity. He longed to have her smile at him in such a way that would soften the lines around her mouth and make her blue eyes glow with affection.

The look of respect and admiration in her eyes sent him reeling. ''A garden's a good thing for a child to have. To eat from the plants that he takes care of. You're a good father, Josh.''

A slow rush of heat spread up his neck. ''Thank you,'' he said quietly.

Awkward silence arced between them. Josh caught his father's knowing, pleased smile and quickly looked away. He didn't want to see the hope flaring behind the amusement.

''When I bought this house, I told Griff he could plant anything he wanted.''

''That's right,'' Griff piped in. ''I chose the green

beans, cantaloupe and watermelon. The corn and the tomatoes were Grandpa's idea.''

''Well, what's a garden without corn or tomatoes?'' Rod interjected.

''When did you buy this place?'' Rachel asked in a tight voice.

Josh shrugged. ''About four years ago.''

Her mouth went slightly slack. Josh waited for her to explain her obvious surprise. Instead, she bit into her bread and concentrated on chewing.

''Dad, after dinner can I show Rachel the pictures of you guys in the attic?''

Her head snapped up.

Josh frowned and shook his head. ''No, I'm sure she isn't interested in going down memory lane. Those pictures are for us, son.''

That Griff knew about the box of pictures tucked away upstairs surprised Josh, and he made a mental note to ask his son how he'd discovered them when he wasn't allowed in the attic. Josh hadn't realized until they'd all moved into this house together that his father had kept Josh's yearbooks and memorabilia from high school, including pictures of him and Rachel.

He noted with interest the flare of curiosity in Rachel's eyes before she averted her gaze and studied her near-empty plate.

As they finished the meal and cleared the table, Rachel touched Rod's arm. ''I'm ready to go.''

Josh leaned against the sink and exchanged a look with his father. ''I'll take you.''

She barely glanced at him. ''I don't think—''

''Dad's eyesight at night isn't what it used to be.'' Josh received a pained look from his father. Though it was true his father did have to wear glasses to drive at night, he could have driven her back, but Josh wanted the opportunity to make sure they agreed on keeping their promise to Mrs. G.

Rachel sent Rod a questioning look. He held up his hands in a gesture of "What can I say?"

Griff bounced from his chair. "Can I go, too, Dad?"

"Yes," Rachel said a little desperately.

"No," Josh said just as quickly.

Griff's gaze swung between the two adults.

"No," Josh repeated. "You need to stay and help Grandpa clean up."

Rod put a hand on Griff's shoulder. "I'll wash, you dry."

Josh opened the door for Rachel. "After you."

Rachel gave Griff a hug. "Thanks for today. I really enjoyed it."

He hugged her back fiercely. "Will I see you before you leave?"

Josh's heart twisted. His son needed a mother. If only— He broke the thought off. God would provide what Griff needed.

As for himself…

Heaven only knew what God had planned for him. But Josh was sure it didn't include Rachel.

Chapter Ten

"I don't know if you'll see me again." Rachel kissed the top of Griff's head and Josh could have sworn she had tears in her eyes. "I'll at least call you to say goodbye if you don't."

Griff smiled sadly. "Okay."

She gave Rod a peck on the cheek. Josh inclined his head as she moved past him and left the house.

"Dad?"

Josh paused. "Yes, son."

"I like Rachel."

His heart stalled for a moment and he nodded, not sure what to say.

Griff cocked his head. "Do you?"

Everything stilled inside Josh. At Griff's intent expression, he stepped closer and knelt down so they were at eye level. The innocently asked question deserved a truthful, uncomplicated answer. "Yes."

"You used to love her, right?"

Josh swallowed as his heart began to thud erratically in his chest. Warily he nodded again.

"Do you still?"

He couldn't go there right now. That question couldn't be answered in uncomplicated terms. "Griff, this isn't the time for this discussion."

"But, Dad, do you?" Griff insisted, his expression earnest and unshakable.

"I...why?"

Griff launched himself at Josh, his small arms encircling his neck. "I don't want her to go." Griff buried his face into Josh's shoulder.

Pain sliced a jagged tear through Josh as he held his son and closed his eyes. He should have seen this coming. He couldn't do anything about what was done, but there was no way he could allow it to happen again.

They would get through this together, he and his son. Just as he and his father had made it through his mother's departure from their lives.

"Shh now." He wiped Griff's tears away. "When I get home we'll talk some more. I need you to be strong now."

Griff nodded. Rod came and placed an arm around the boy's shoulders as Josh stood. "You go on. Rachel's waiting. We'll be just fine, won't we, Griff?"

Wiping at his nose, Griff mumbled, "Sure."

With a heavy heart Josh left the house. He was determined to protect his son, even if it meant breaking his promise to Mrs. G.

Rachel pushed away from the truck and allowed Josh to unlock the passenger door. She noticed there was a distance in his eyes that hadn't been there before, and tiny lines framed the corners of his mouth.

She climbed into the cab. With a decisive snap he shut the door he'd held open for her. She flinched.

In the setting sun, she watched him walk around the front of the truck. His honey-blond hair shone in the sun's waning rays and her heart skipped a beat. He was handsome in a rugged, outdoorsy sort of way that she found very appealing.

Since the moment he'd walked into the kitchen in his ranger's uniform, she'd been having trouble remembering that nothing good would come of getting close to him. Instead, her fanciful mind skipped off with thoughts of what it would be like to live in that house and wait for him to come home from work every night. In the house he *hadn't* shared with Andrea.

She couldn't explain why that news had sent such pleasure ricocheting through her.

Josh climbed in and started the engine. He eased the truck out of the driveway and onto the road. They rode in unsettling silence until Rachel couldn't stand it. "You've done a fine job with Griff."

"So you said," he replied tersely.

They lapsed back into silence. Where was the fun and teasing man she'd spent the day with?

"Rachel."

His tone set her on wary alert. She studied his profile. His jaw tightened into a grim line. She waited. The silence stretched out. She watched his expression shift ever so slightly, as if he was struggling for the words. Finally he let out a quick breath. "I can't do this."

His words were so quiet, she might have missed what he'd said if she hadn't been anticipating something. "What can't you do?"

He took a deep breath and exhaled slowly. "I'm not going to be able to keep my promise. Not at the expense of my son."

She blinked. "I don't understand."

"Griff's the most important thing in my life. I have to protect my son."

"What do you have to protect him from?" She held her breath, not sure where he was going with this.

"I have to protect him from you."

She drew back, stung. "Me? You're not making sense."

"He likes you and he's becoming too attached to you. Today wasn't a good idea. It would be best if you kept your distance from him until you leave."

His words were a slap across the face. What had she done to warrant such a warning? She quickly thought back over the day. Nothing justified Josh's attitude. She liked Griff and the boy liked her. What was wrong with that?

She stared at Josh in speculation. Why was he reacting like this? Did Josh think Griff wouldn't understand why she had to go back to Chicago? "I think you underestimate your son. I explained to him about my leaving. He understands why I can't stay."

"You've discussed this with him?" His voice sounded strained.

"Yes. He's a sweet child and I was touched he'd want to have me as a mother, but we talked about why that was impossible and he understood the situation."

Josh slowed the truck and pulled to the side of the road. He gripped the steering wheel tightly. "He asked you to be his *mother?*"

Uh-oh. She shouldn't have said anything. But he should know what was going on inside his son's head. "Well, yes. Though I think his asking has more to do with losing Mom G. than with me. A boy needs a mother, and he's just lost the only mother figure he's known."

Josh's jaw tightened, and his displeasure surged toward her in waves. She empathized with his need to safeguard his son's well-being, but Josh also had to understand that the boy needed more in his life. "Griff's starved for female attention. You know what it's like to grow up without a mother."

"I turned out fine," he said between clenched teeth.

"Like you're not full of anger and bitterness," she tossed out, shaking her head in disbelief. "I know how hard it was on you to grow up without your mother."

His eyes narrowed, and the angles in his face hardened. She wondered why he didn't crack under the strain of controlling his temper.

"We're talking about Griff," he grated out, the words harsh and low. "I don't want you to break his heart."

She exhaled a breath in exasperation. "I'm not going to break his heart. Why would you think I'd do such a thing?"

"Because you're good at it," he barked. "Really, really good at it."

Rachel gaped. "Excuse me? I think you need a history lesson, buddy."

"Yeah, right. You're the one who left me, remember?"

"Whoa." She held up a hand. She couldn't believe

he had the audacity to suggest she'd broken his heart. "You knew from the day you met me where my life was headed."

He stared out the front window, his expression no less hard than before.

She should let it drop and leave as quickly as possible, and never look back. She knew she should. But she couldn't. She always met a challenge head-on. "You knew I wanted to be a doctor, but you thought our love should be enough for me. Sorry to burst your bubble. This is the twenty-first century, Josh. Women aren't expected to be content barefoot, pregnant and in the kitchen. Your archaic ideas of what a wife and mother should be need an update."

Josh closed his eyes as if in pain. If what she'd said got him thinking, then the twinge of guilt she felt for hurting him was worth the price.

"You need a wake-up call. If not for yourself, then for Griff. I dread thinking Griff will grow up believing that women shouldn't have a life outside of family. I don't want Griff to end up alone and lonely like his father."

He flinched, and with a little shock, she realized that was exactly how she saw Josh. Alone and lonely, a lot like her, yet he was so stubborn that he probably didn't realize how miserable he was.

She didn't want to care, fought against the softening in her heart. The tiny corner where her teenage fantasies lived seemed to expand, making her chest hurt. Letting any amount of feeling grow was not smart.

And she was a smart woman.

So why did she find it so hard to stop the unwanted emotions from bouncing around, wreaking havoc with her resolve not to care, not to wish there were some way she could help him to find happiness?

He faced her, his expression haggard. "What's wrong with wanting to be the priority in someone's life?"

She sighed. "Nothing. I'm sure Andrea fit the bill perfectly."

He froze, the light of anger in his eyes turned into a raging inferno. "I don't want to talk about her."

Rachel regretted her biting words that stirred up his grief. "I'm sorry. That was uncalled for. I wish you luck in finding the next perfect woman."

"I'm not looking for perfection. I want someone whose priority will be her family. I want..." He shook his head and made a dismissive gesture with his hand. "It doesn't matter."

It doesn't matter. She stiffened. He might as well have said, "you don't matter." Because what he wanted they both knew she couldn't deliver. "My career's my priority. It will always be my priority. It has to be. I have no choice. Can't you see that?"

He surprised her by running a knuckle gently down her cheek, the heat of his touch like a brand.

"I do see. But at what cost?"

"Cost?" She drew away from him. "There's no cost. This is what God wants of me. Making a difference is what my life's about. Why can't you understand that?"

"But life has so much more to offer than work. I can't believe that's all God has planned for you."

His words brought reverberations of her conversation with Mom G. slamming into her consciousness. She hated the little flutter of...hope...battering around her heart because it threatened her career. But more importantly, she wanted to believe in the hope. "'More' as in you?"

He sat back, his hands once again tightly gripping the steering wheel. "No."

That one simple word sliced through her like an out-of-control surgeon slicing a vital organ with a scalpel. Swallowing a gasp of pain, she stared at his strong profile. Shadows deepened the contours and accentuated the angles. Her heart bled.

"No, I am quite aware that the time we've shared these past few days has led us to a dead end," he stated, his tone less harsh. "'More' as in enjoying life. Where's the joy in your life?"

She closed her eyes against the certainty that there would never be a future for them and asked, "What makes you think I don't enjoy my life?"

Staring straight ahead, he sighed. "Your intentions are honorable, I'll give you that."

She opened her eyes and raised her chin. "But…?"

He turned to stare at her, his eyes burning like hot coals in the dark. "There are other ways of making a difference."

"Not for me. There's no other option." She couldn't go against what God wanted, any more than she could stop breathing.

Without further comment he started the engine and drove to the hotel. She was thankful for the reprieve from her own torturous thoughts, and when the truck swung into the parking lot, she had the door partly opened before they came to a stop. She hopped out and turned to say goodbye. Discomfited, she watched Josh open his door and climb out.

"You don't have to walk me to the door, Josh. This isn't a date." She walked past him and up the stairs.

He stopped at the foot of the steps. "You're right, Rachel, this isn't a date. It's a goodbye."

Her heart twisted at the finality in his words. But saying goodbye now was for the best. She didn't think her heart could stand this emotional upheaval anymore. She wanted her nice, controlled existence back. Wanted to be back where she knew what was what and had everything lined up with no risk of heartache. She needed the detachment that had served her well over the years. With supreme effort, she managed to sound cool. "Goodbye."

Josh crossed his arms over his broad chest. "You'll let me know how you're doing when you get back?"

She arched a brow. "I thought you'd decided you couldn't keep your promise?"

"Not while you're in town."

Her gaze lifted away from him standing there so closed off, and settled on the half-moon high in the sky. "I see."

But she didn't really. Was he having as much trouble keeping his heart from aching for her as she was for him? A small wry laugh escaped. Who was she kidding? Josh had made it abundantly clear he didn't want her. Two days at the most and she could resume her life. "Goodbye, Josh." She fumbled for her key.

Josh approached and she braced herself.

He laid a hot hand on her shoulder. "I didn't mean to hurt your feelings."

She closed her eyes against the soul-searing pain of his touch. "You didn't."

The denial rang false as she sniffed back tears. Where was her composure, her resolve not to allow him to affect her? She'd been away from her job too long. She wasn't herself. This person who always seemed on the verge of tears wasn't her. She feared she'd lose her effectiveness as a doctor if this penchant for emotions continued. She didn't want to feel. She didn't want to want him.

He turned her around. "Rachel, I'm sorry."

She wouldn't ever be able to forget him. He'd always been in her life, a shadowy figure that other men had fallen short of. Too bad it had taken until today for her to realize it. All this time she hadn't wanted him to take root in her heart when he'd already been there. Angry with him, angry with herself, her temper rose. "Sorry you made a promise you don't want to keep?"

His gaze narrowed before his face settled into that neutral expression she hated. He stepped back. The two-foot distance between them seemed as wide as California. He didn't deny her accusations, didn't defend himself. "God go with you, Rachel. I hope you find peace in your life."

He walked down the stairs and was halfway to his truck before she managed to react. How dare he be magnanimous and wish her well. She'd find peace all right. God would see to that. *As long as you aren't in my life, Josh Taylor, I'll be just fine.*

As she watched him drive his truck away, she prayed she wasn't deluding herself. She *would* be fine without Josh Taylor. She had to be.

The next morning as she watched the moving van being loaded with the items she'd chosen to keep, stark reality hit. With Mom G.'s passing, she mattered to no one. Rachel was truly on her own.

Who would claim any of her possessions as mementos of her life when she was gone? Sadly, no one.

No one who would care. No one would mourn her passing. A desolate and vacant hole formed in her heart, making her acutely aware of how alone in life she really was.

After the van disappeared down the driveway, she entered the house to stare at the piles of stuff that would be donated to Goodwill.

So many things accumulated over a lifetime and yet, what value did possessions really have? Mom G. would be in heaven now; her reward for living a life expressing Jesus' love would be a beautiful crown with many jewels upon her head. One of those jewels would be for Rachel, for taking in and loving an unwanted child.

What treasure was she laying for herself up in heaven? Saving the lives of people she didn't know and didn't love? There was merit in her work. But where was the love?

The stillness of the house, the tomblike quiet, made Rachel edgy. Even the exercises that normally calmed her mind and body did little to offer rest for her harried thoughts. She missed Griff, missed his generous affection and easy laughter.

She could admit that easily enough, though thoughts of Griff always led back to Josh. To the miniscule area that harbored feelings that weren't wanted. To his stubborn refusal to give an inch toward accepting her need to be a doctor.

She resigned herself to knowing he would never comprehend what her career meant to her. And she accepted that Josh wasn't to be a part of her life.

The next day, after the Goodwill truck had left and Mom G.'s house was empty, Rachel returned to her hotel. Restless, and needing to get out of the quiet hotel room, she donned the running shoes she'd packed and set out.

She worked up a sweat running on the country roads that wound around the town of Sonora. Her lungs filled with the smog-free air and her senses took in the scenic tranquillity of the verdant trees, foliage and quaint homes along the way.

She ran for hours, occasionally slowing to a walk to sip from the water bottle attached to her fanny pack, before resuming her heart-pounding pace, trying to outrun the memory of Josh's goodbye.

Late in the afternoon, with muscles quivering, Rachel's pace became a brisk stroll as she talked with God, asking for wisdom and guidance. *Josh, doesn't want me and I can't walk away from the work I'm doing. Lord, I don't understand. What is it You want from me?*

Her heart beat wildly though the adrenaline from her run had long dissipated. She felt as if she stood on the brink of understanding and one little nudge…

She raised her gaze heavenward hoping for enlightenment and noticed that in the distance a discernible gray trail of smoke wound its way toward the sky. She frowned. Fire season had started early this year.

The beep of a horn drew her attention. Rod's Buick pulled to the side of the street. He gestured to her.

"Hi." The pleasure of seeing a friendly face gladdened her heart.

"Griff's in trouble," Rod stated tersely.

Apprehension uncoiled in her veins. "What's wrong?"

"He got separated from his Boy Scout troop. They

went hiking up at the lake and I'm worried." Rod pointed toward the front window.

She lifted her gaze toward the rising smoke over the mountain ridge. Her heart pounded in her ears. "He's out there?"

Rod nodded. "Will you come?"

Without answering she opened the door and climbed in. *Dear Lord, put Your angels around Griff and keep him safe.*

As the car sped away, Rachel tried not to think what would happen to Josh if he lost Griff, too.

Josh stared at the map hanging on the wall of the ranger's station conference room. Several red thumbtacks stuck out, indicating the locations of his crews. They'd been working furiously to contain the sudden heat fire that engulfed the woods around Cherry Lake.

He hated to think of the damage being done. The acres of trees and wildlife being destroyed. Beyond the destruction of the forest, he knew the fire might cause human fatality. The beauty of the lake attracted day hikers and backpackers alike. The search and res cue teams had been deployed.

These situations were never good when people could be trapped. Families out for the day, overnight hikers, scout troops—thank goodness Griff's troop went to Pine Mountain Lake today—and teens. Teens like he and Rachel had been, seeking privacy for hot kisses and carving names into trees. Hopefully the fire wouldn't destroy their tree. He grimaced at the use of the pronoun. There was no "their" anymore.

Back when life had seemed full of possibilities, they'd found a plateau overlooking the lake where a lone oak tree stood. Their spot, their tree. He'd carved their initials into the trunk.

The memory was bittersweet. He shook his head. He had no business letting thoughts of Rachel crowd his mind. They'd said their goodbyes. He doubted they'd see or hear from her again.

Explaining to his son why he wouldn't be seeing her again had been one of the hardest things Josh had ever done. Confessing to his boy that he'd basically forbid Rachel to have any more contact with Griff had put a wedge between father and son.

Josh could have blamed Rachel, could have told his son that she didn't keep her promises, but he couldn't. Not only was that untrue, but for reasons he refused to examine, he'd preferred his son be angry with him rather than with Rachel.

Griff would get over his anger and they'd repair their relationship. Someday he hoped Griff would understand why not having Rachel in their lives was for the best. Someday Josh would tell his son to be careful when he fell in love. He didn't want Griff to make the same mistake of finding someone who would only commit to one thing—her career.

Rachel had called him chauvinistic. Was it chauvinistic to want to be loved passionately? To want to know that the woman he loved wouldn't up and leave one day? He just wanted a wife whose love he would be sure of. He would never be sure of Rachel's feelings because her devotion to medicine was all consuming. And even understanding her belief that she was doing God's will didn't make letting her go any easier. It made him admire her for her faith and obedience, and made him aware of his unworthiness to receive anything from God.

A commotion in the outer office brought his mind back to the problem at hand. Abruptly he turned from the wall and headed out of the conference room into the large lobby of the log-cabin-style ranger's station. He stopped short.

Amid the chaos of people doing their jobs stood Rachel, wearing nylon jogging shorts and a tank top, talking quickly and gesturing wildly to Joe Leads, Timber Manager

"What are you doing here, Rachel?"

At the sound of his voice her attention snapped to him. Her big blue eyes looked panicked.

Warily Josh moved toward her as she rushed to him. What would make her seek him out? Dread knotted his muscles. What would make her lose her control?

Chapter Eleven

She grabbed his arm, her grasp fierce and biting. "Josh, you have to come quick."

Josh frowned. Concern overrode the shock of seeing her again. He fought it back. "Rachel, we're in the middle of fighting a fire—"

"Griff's out there," she gasped.

Fear, stark and choking, seized Josh's heart, but he tried to rationalize it away. "They're miles from the fire. His troop went to Pine Mountain Lake."

"No. Rod said there'd been a last-minute change in plans and he dropped Griff off at Cherry Lake this morning." Cool, collected Rachel sounded scared. "The troop leader called and said Griff and another boy got separated from the group. Your dad went in after them."

For a dizzying moment Josh fought the panic threatening to cut off his air supply. The world narrowed down to one terrorizing thought: *I can't lose Griff, too.*

He recovered his equilibrium and forced his mind

to concentrate on what needed to be done. In long strides he crossed the room, grabbed his keys and coat. "Connie, call George. Tell him what's happening. Tell him I'm going in to find my son and that my dad's on his way in.

"Joe, you take over here and call the sheriff's department with this update. See if they've already located Griff. Call me on my cell." He shouted the commands as he grabbed two walkie-talkies from a cabinet. His heart pounded in his ears, but he kept moving, kept focused on the details.

"You, Chris—" he pointed to a startled young ranger "—you're going in with me."

"But he hasn't—" Joe began.

Josh cut him off with a glare. "I need you here." He stated the obvious. Joe nodded sharply, acknowledging one of the prime rules: Go in with a buddy.

Josh hurried toward the door with Chris right on his heels. He didn't even stop when he heard Rachel's cry of "What about me?"

"Go home," he growled over his shoulder, and then he was out the door.

Rachel stared at the door as it slammed shut behind Josh's retreating back. *Go home.* Like she could go home now. Not with Griff missing and a fire blazing. Her feet were moving before she'd even thought about commanding them to. She rushed out the door and watched Josh's truck speeding away.

She ignored the bite of rejection at Josh's harsh command and ran for Rod's Buick. *He's going to need you, Rachel. Whatever happens today, Josh is going to need you.* Rod's words echoed inside her head as she drove after Josh.

Yeah, well, tell him *that, why don't you?* she

thought sourly. She pressed harder on the gas pedal. The Buick shook with the speed, but she didn't let up as she turned off Highway 120 and headed up the gravel road that would lead her to the lake.

Josh's truck had long since disappeared ahead of her. But she knew where he'd start. Not at the usual visitors' trailhead. No, he'd take the fire road until it ended miles up the trail. She didn't question her certainty, she just knew. She almost missed the turn for the fire road but the faint cloud of dust clinging to the air pointed the way.

Josh and Chris were already out of sight by the time she parked the Buick behind Josh's truck. A fallen log blocked the way. They'd have to hike up the fire road to where it converged with the main trail. She ran to catch up to them, grimacing at the awful smell of smoke. Her approaching footsteps gave away her arrival before she had thought of what to say.

Josh's head whipped around, his eyes widened for a fraction of a second before narrowing to burning slits. "Go back, Rachel. I don't want you here. You'll just get in the way."

Her heart tore at the pain visible beneath his obvious irritation. "You might need me. I'm a doctor, remember."

His feet still moved at a rapid pace—she had to take three steps to his one—but his eyes remained on her for a long moment. His lip curled into a nasty sneer. "A city doctor."

"A doctor just the same," she retorted between gulps of air, the smoke burning her lungs. "I'm coming with you. Get over it."

"Rachel, you're a civilian. I—"

"Which means you can't order me around," she interrupted tersely.

He snorted at her over his shoulder, his pace never slowing. "If you think you can handle it."

She noticed Chris kept glancing at her but she didn't feel inclined to appease his curiosity.

Being behind the two men, Rachel got a good dose of dust kicked up into her face. She tried to stifle her coughs because every time she coughed loud enough for Josh to hear, he'd turn and glare at her. She could feel his animosity toward her, claiming he found her presence a nuisance. But Griff was the one out there, maybe hurt, needing help. And if she could help, then angering Josh was a small price to pay.

When the fire road met with the main trail, Josh stopped abruptly. Chris smoothly sidestepped him, but Rachel had her head down and didn't realize he'd stopped until she ran smack into his broad back, knocking her off her feet.

She glared up him. He stared back dispassionately.

"You could help me up," she groused, her bottom aching from the impact with the ground.

For a tense moment Rachel thought he wouldn't help her. Finally he stuck out a hand and swiftly pulled her to her feet. He dropped her hand quickly and turned to Chris. "Take the trail down to the visitors' center. You should meet my father. When you do, contact me." He turned a knob on one of the walkie-talkies before handing it over to the bemused youth.

"I thought we were to stay together?" Chris questioned, his young face creasing with anxiety.

Josh flipped the knobs on his own walkie-talkie. "Take her with you."

"No," Rachel said immediately. If Griff or the other boy were hurt… She didn't even want to think about that. They had to find the two boys before it got dark.

"It's safer if you go with Chris," he replied without looking at her.

Anger that he'd dismiss her so readily gave her words a cutting edge. "Safer for whom?"

He glanced at her sharply. Then gave a wry twist of his lips. "For both of us." With that left between them, he turned and headed up the trail.

Rachel stared after him for a moment, wondering what he meant by that remark. Then she turned to the kid beside her. "You go on, Chris. I'll stay with Josh."

At the young man's hesitancy, she nodded. "It's okay. Go find Rod."

Chris shrugged and headed in the opposite direction. Rachel trudged after Josh. She wasn't sure if he knew that she followed several feet behind him, until his voice came at her tight and clipped. "You could easily make it back to the car before dark."

"I'm coming with you," she declared through ragged breaths.

"Suit yourself," he grumbled.

A dull ache throbbed in her side. She ignored her fatigued body's protest against the extra exercise.

The trail narrowed. Tree branches brushed across her legs, biting into her skin. Wryly she glanced down at her slick running shoes, made for smooth paved track, not rugged dirt trails. Her gaze lifted to Josh. His uniform and work boots were much better suited for the trek.

They hiked to the clanking rhythm of Josh's fire ax

hanging from his gear belt. The smoke grew thicker by the minute. In the distance she could hear the crackling and hissing of trees burning. Somewhere out there men were fighting the fire. Somewhere out there was Griff.

Josh stopped in his tracks. Rachel ran headfirst into his back again. He put out a steadying hand. "Pay attention," he snapped.

He called for Griff, his voice loud and booming through the trees. They waited, but only the sounds of the flaming forest answered.

He started forward again. Rachel followed, aware of the fear in Josh's eyes, aware of the panic building within her chest. She'd been panicked when she'd arrived at the station, but once she'd seen Josh, the panic had given way to an assurance that he would make things right. He'd find his son and the world would go on. It shook her to the core to see Josh so scared.

The third time Josh stopped abruptly, Rachel managed not to ram into him. Her tennis shoes skidded on the loose dirt, raising a murky cloud of dust.

Their fruitless cries for Griff echoed back at them through the tree. Josh's gaze traveled over her with concern. "You're not dressed for this."

"I didn't plan on going for a hike in the wilderness today." She tried for some levity, but failed.

He rubbed a hand over his face. "I should have grabbed some gear out of the truck for you. I wasn't thinking."

She caught his hand in hers. "You were worried about Griff. Besides, you didn't know I'd follow you."

Josh's gaze moved away from her and to the

wooded trail. ''He should have been headed back down by now. He knows how to pace himself, how to gauge his time and distance so that at any given point he could turn back and know exactly how much time the return would take.'' He held her hand tightly. ''What am I going to do if anything happens to my son?'' His voice was ragged and his face in the dusky light showed the signs of the terrible thoughts running through his head.

''Josh, don't. You can't assume anything. We'll find him. We have to trust that God will protect him.''

''I know. I know. But the fire…''

''Remember what you asked me in the hospital? You asked if I trusted God. Now, I'm asking you, Josh. Do you trust Him? Is your faith strong enough?''

She held her breath. The last time she'd asked he'd seemed to struggle for his answer. On some level, she knew he was at a turning point in his relationship with God. Choosing to trust when things were going your way was easy, but trusting in the midst of a crisis, when only the Almighty was in control, took a step in faith.

'''Faith's being sure of what we hope for and certain of what we do not see,''' she quoted softly.

He closed his eyes. Rachel could only guess he was searching his own heart for the answer, desperately trying not to let his fear overwhelm him. He breathed out and his eyes opened.

They were clearer, less panicked, more focused. ''I do trust Him.''

He held out his other hand. Rachel slipped her free hand into his. She garnered comfort from his touch.

He bowed his head and prayed aloud, a simple, heartfelt plea for God's protection and direction.

When he'd finished, he slipped out of his jacket and wrapped it around her shoulders. "Thank you, Rachel."

She looked up at him in surprise. "I should be the one thanking you for the coat."

In the fading light she saw a soft smile curve his lips. "Thank you for reminding me where my strength lies."

His smile made her heart quicken. His eyes, hot with intensity, locked with hers. She swallowed.

A static beep drew their attention, breaking the momentary spell.

"Son, come in." Rod's voice came from the little box that Josh had secured to his belt.

He grabbed the instrument. "Copy, Dad."

"Have you found them?"

"Negative, Dad. We're almost to the summit and we'll head down to the shoreline."

"We'll head toward you then." Rod's voice sounded strained.

Josh frowned. "Copy, Dad. Be careful."

"You too, son. Take care of Rachel, too."

"Copy that, Dad. Out."

"Will your dad be okay?" Rachel asked, thinking about Rod's age and Josh's frown.

"Yes. He has years of experience and Chris with him. They'll be fine. How about you? How are you doing?"

Her feet hurt and her muscles were cramping, but adrenaline kept the pain from overwhelming her. "I'm fine. Let's keep moving."

His expression said he didn't quite believe her, but

he gave a sharp nod and they continued on. Rachel noticed that Josh adjusted his stride so she didn't have to jog.

She knew what that little concession must cost him in anxiety. She could feel his restrained power as his long legs ate up the ground beside her. Soon they reached the top of the small summit where the trail began to head down toward the lake.

The sight stole her breath. On the far side of the lake the fire burned hot and bright. Tall trees glowing like eerie specters rising from the ground sent a shiver sliding over her arms. Standing at the top like this, the smoke was thick and burning to her lungs.

Below them the water reflected the red glow of the flames, making the blaze overwhelming. Where could Griff be? Surely at this frightening sight he'd have headed back, unless he were hurt. Her throat constricted at the thought.

Josh yelled for Griff and she added her own cries to his. Their voices echoed across the water. Below, nothing moved; there wasn't any sign of life.

"Where could they be?" she wondered aloud, her eyes scanning the darkness.

"I don't know. Unless—" He broke off. His gaze traveling from the lake to the left, down an incline to the plateau where the top of an oak tree jutted out above the other trees.

She followed his gaze. "The tree?"

"Maybe." He looked thoughtful. "Worth a chance."

The implication that he'd told Griff about their tree left her reeling. The memories of that last visit to the old oak were etched firmly in her heart. It was the day she'd told Josh goodbye. Leaving him had been the hardest thing she'd ever done.

They left the trail and started down the hill. Rocks slid beneath Rachel's feet. Josh grabbed her arm and steadied her. As they neared the bottom, Josh yelled for Griff again.

A faint noise from below them paused Rachel's heart. Josh halted and called again. An answering cry filled the air. Spurred on by the tiny voice, she scrambled behind Josh. As they came out of the brush and into the clearing, a small boy came running forward. "Mr. Taylor."

Josh ran to the dark-haired boy and gathered him in his arms. "Ben, are you okay? Where's Griff?"

She watched as he checked the boy for injuries. Josh's compassion for the frightened child touched her deeply.

Ben dissolved into tears, and Josh put his big, strong arms around the small boy. "Shh, it's all right. You're safe now. Where's Griff?"

Over the boy's head Rachel met his gaze. She saw fear, stark and vivid, in his hazel eyes. She stepped closer and laid a hand on his shoulder.

Ben gulped, his body shaking. "He—he fell. I didn't know what to do. I didn't want to leave him. And the fire…the forest's b-burning."

"Show me where Griff is," Josh said in a tight, strained voice.

The boy took Josh's hand and pulled him toward the lone tree. Rachel saw two legs jutting out from the other side. The side that bore the marks that Josh had carved into the trunk. Was that what lured him from his troop?

Quickly they rounded the tree and stopped short.

Griff lay prone and still. Rachel rushed past a frozen Josh to kneel at Griff's side. She fought a moment of alarm and forced her mind to focus. She immediately checked his pulse, which was strong, his breathing and then searched for injuries.

Josh knelt down beside her and very carefully took Griff's hand. "Griff, Griff." His voice broke.

"He's breathing and his heartbeat's good," she said.

"He's alive," Josh breathed out, his relief evident.

"Yes, he's alive." She laid a reassuring hand on his arm and blinked back sudden tears. She gained control of herself and turned to the boy. "Ben, how long has he been unconscious?" Her tone was amazingly cool, despite the hammering in her chest.

"I—I don't know. For a while." The boy burst into fresh tears.

She looked up to see Josh staring at her intently. "His ankle's swollen, probably broken. He has a contusion on his head. We need to get him out of here."

"I'll carry him back." Josh moved to pick up his son.

Rachel squeezed his arm tightly. "You need to call for the rescue team to come take him out on a backboard."

"No. That will take too long. You said he was okay, just a broken ankle."

"Josh, my evaluation's superficial. We won't know if he has internal injuries until we can get him to the hospital. You could do more damage by moving him."

Her stern and uncompromising tone rang with familiarity in her own ears. This was the voice that got things done in the E.R. How easily and comfortably she slipped back into her doctor persona.

She could see he didn't want to comply with her assessment, but after a moment's hesitation, he acquiesced. From the pocket of the coat that she'd laid over Griff he pulled out a cellular phone and dialed. He quickly and tersely explained their situation.

Next he grabbed his walkie-talkie. "Dad, come in."

"Here, son. Have you found Griff?" Rod's voice sounded breathless.

"Yes. Where are you?"

"Just cresting the summit now."

"Take the incline to your left. We're here. Griff's unconscious, but alive. Rachel wants us to wait to move him. I've called for the rescue team. They should arrive shortly."

"Copy that, thank God. Out."

"Copy, out." He turned to her, his expression grim and full of worry. "What can we do?"

"Wait." The one word that was so hard to do. Part of the practice of medicine consisted of waiting and seeing. Sometimes God worked miracles where a doctor never could.

Josh stood and paced. "How did he fall, Ben?"

"He was trying to climb the tree."

Josh groaned. "He knows better than to do that by himself. How many times have I told him that without supervision he could get hurt?"

"He's a boy exploring his world, Josh," she stated quietly.

He whirled on her. "What do you know about it? You're not a parent."

She drew back at his angry outburst, hurt by his harsh words.

Immediately his expression turned contrite. "I'm sorry. That was uncalled for. I didn't mean—"

She held up a hand. "You're right, Josh. I'm not a parent. I can only imagine the torment you're feeling right now."

Though she'd only known Griff a short time, she loved the boy and had felt the same fear as Josh. She'd glimpsed the battle Josh fought every day with fear, the fear that something would happen to his son, one of the risks of family she wasn't sure she was up for. She forgave him his painful words. But the sting reminded her she wasn't welcome in Josh's life.

The sound of voices carrying down the hill was a welcome relief. Rod and Chris charged through the brush, quickly followed by three uniformed rescue personnel. Josh hastily detailed the situation.

"They snuck away from the rest of the troop and came up the hill from the shoreline," Rod explained to Rachel as he came to kneel by Griff's feet.

A member of the rescue team knelt beside Rachel. She gave him her evaluation. The man, named Brian, placed a neck brace on Griff. The other two members of the team brought over a backboard.

Efficiently they secured Griff to the board and splinted his ankle, then lifted him and cautiously headed up the hill. Rachel picked up Josh's jacket and watched as Josh disappeared with the rescue team.

Rod's arm came around her shoulders. "Shall we?"

She nodded, feeling suddenly exhausted. They followed Chris and Ben up the hill moving at a good clip.

"There'll be an ambulance meeting us at the fire road," Rod explained.

"That's good."

"Thanks for staying with Josh. I know he appreciated your presence."

Rachel gave Rod a sidelong glance. "I probably slowed him down."

Rod shrugged. "You two worked together and found Griff. That's what matters."

They'd worked together. Like a team. A couple. The pang that thought brought made Rachel stumble. Rod's hand on her arm steadied her. They weren't a couple. She would be leaving in the morning, going back to her life where she needed to stay focused on her goal. But the enthusiasm for the task didn't come, didn't fill her with the peace it usually did.

Rod cleared his throat. "You know, Josh still needs you."

"Hardly."

"The fire's still blazing. He's got a job to do. He's going to need your help."

Rod's softly spoken words echoed inside her head. "My help?"

"With Griff, while he fights the fire."

She doubted Josh would recant his demand for her to stay away from his son. He hadn't wanted her to come on the search. He surely wouldn't want her to stay with Griff. "They have you."

"I'm needed out here, too. We're going to need every hand available to stop this blaze."

In anxiety-ridden silence, Rachel digested her conversation with Rod. Josh had needed her, but did he still? *Lord, show me what to do.*

At the head of the fire road, lights blazed. Two

people came rushing forward from one of the vehicles.

"Ben!" called Ben's mother. Ben hurried to meet his parents.

Rachel smiled to see the three hugging and kissing. Until recently, she hadn't known what that would feel like. To be so glad to see someone, to hold them close and be thankful for their existence.

But she'd felt that with Griff. She loved Josh's son, and she intended to continue to be there for him somehow, some way. Even if that meant staying a few days longer in Josh's world where she wasn't welcome.

Chapter Twelve

With Rod at her side, she headed toward his car.

"Rachel." Josh's voice brought her to a halt. He stood at the open doors to the ambulance. Inside, a paramedic worked on Griff. She knew he'd hook him up to an IV to keep him hydrated.

"Go on," Rod urged.

She moved forward on wooden feet. "Yes?"

"Ride with us," Josh said abruptly.

She was astonished by Josh's request and by the thrilling glow that flowed through her in response. "Of course." She climbed in and sat on the narrow bench next to Griff. She heard Josh tell his dad they'd see him at the hospital. The two men hugged. Josh climbed in and sat next to her.

When he gathered her hand in his, her brows rose in stunned surprise. Heat embraced her palm and traveled to her heart, making her aware of Josh's close proximity and of the need she felt in his touch. He *did* need her for Griff's sake.

"Thank you for being here." His voice was thick and unsteady.

Her heart went out to him and a calming peace settled over her. "You're welcome."

What would he think when he learned that she intended to keep her promise to Mom G., and that for the next few days it wasn't going to be from long distance?

"Can't you go any faster?" Josh grumbled, anxiety twisting in his chest.

"We're going as fast as we can, sir," the ambulance driver replied with curt politeness.

Josh stared at his unconscious son. He looked so little and helpless lying on the backboard. Love swelled to overwhelming proportions, making Josh aware of how vulnerable his heart was where his son was concerned. If he lost Griff, he didn't know if he could survive life in one piece.

Do you trust Him? Rachel had asked. Such a simple question yet not easily answered.

In placing his trust in the Lord, Josh was admitting he had no control over life. No control over whether his son lived or died. The out-of-control feeling nagged at his soul with frightening intensity. He'd had to call on every bit of knowledge he possessed about God to say yes with any conviction.

God was not some powerful being who took joy in His creations' pain, but rather a Heavenly Father who suffered with His children.

Faith, Rachel had reminded him, was more than just believing. Faith was trusting in something intangible, placing your life in God's care and being assured that He would work all things out for your own good.

The comforting pressure of Rachel's hand in his reminded him of her presence. He looked up to meet her gentle, blue gaze. There was nothing icy in the subtle look of understanding in her eyes.

This woman amazed him. She'd been there for him when he needed her quiet strength, her steady, reassuring presence. She'd kept her cool. Her doctorly, professional cool. And he was grateful.

Why she had insisted on coming to help search for Griff, he could only guess at the answer. He supposed the bond she and his son had formed had prompted her assistance.

Any other reason… He wouldn't go there, couldn't go there. Surely her determination to help had only stemmed from her love of his son and her experience as a doctor, not from feelings for him. Yet, as he held her gaze, he couldn't stop the ache that suddenly consumed his heart.

To divert his uneasy thoughts, he said, "You think he'll be okay?"

Her expression didn't change. "The fracture in his ankle seems to be a clean break but only an X ray will tell for certain."

His gaze moved to the purple bruise on Griff's forehead. "What about his head?"

"Head injuries are tricky. We won't know what damage, if any, he has sustained until we run tests and he wakes up. But the size of the lump and the location indicate to me that at worst he may have a pretty good concussion. The forehead's the thickest part of the skull."

Her soft voice worked like a balm to his tightly

strung nerves. Just as she'd calmly soothed his panic when they'd found Griff and for that agonizing moment when he'd thought his son was dead.

"I froze." The admission tore from him.

She blinked. "What?"

He couldn't meet her gaze now. If he saw disdain in her eyes it would kill him. But he needed to get the words out. His self-loathing wouldn't permit him not to. "I froze. I saw him lying there and couldn't function."

He rubbed the back of his neck. "Even though I know what to do. I've been trained by the best. I've worked Search and Rescue. But when it mattered the most, I froze."

"Don't blame yourself, Josh." With her free hand, she drew his face toward her. When he met her gaze, he didn't see the reproach he'd anticipated. Instead he saw understanding and compassion.

"When it's someone you love who's hurt, it makes a difference. I can't tell you how many times I've seen the most competent doctors turn into a mass of jelly when their child or spouse is injured. Don't beat yourself up about something that happens to everyone in your situation. Doctors don't treat their own for that precise reason."

He wanted to believe her. To believe *in* her. Her hand stroked his cheek. He'd willingly endure frostbite for her precious touch. He pressed a kiss to her palm. Her eyes widened but she didn't withdraw. "Thank you," he whispered.

Her tender smile sent a deep yearning screaming through his tension-filled body. A yearning for what could never be: Rachel loving him and being his wife.

Rachel's career was important to her, so important

he couldn't ask her to give it up. And he knew she never would for him.

He frowned at the turn of his thoughts. She dropped her hand away and loosened her hold on him, as if giving him a chance to withdraw if he wanted. He tightened his hold.

He didn't want to go through this alone. He didn't like living a life by himself, not having someone to share the heartache and the joy with. He wanted a helpmate. He wanted Rachel, needed her, if only for now.

He forced his thoughts away from dangerous ground and onto the one love that he was sure of— his son.

What had Griff been thinking, wandering off from the troop like that? And going to that tree? He glanced up at Rachel. Their tree. Her eyes were trained on Griff, but she was miles away, lost in her thoughts.

"You know, I have no idea how Griff knew about the tree," he said softly.

Her brows rose in response to his statement but she didn't turn toward him.

"Dad could have told him," Josh said aloud, more to keep the silence from filling his head with far-fetched thoughts he had no business thinking than from wanting any more of a response from her.

Thoughts like how much he admired and respected Rachel for pursuing her dreams, even at the cost to him, and about how good a doctor she must be if what he'd glimpsed today was any indication. She'd known what to do, had been efficient, yet caring.

When they arrived at the hospital, Josh jumped out before the vehicle stopped completely. Rachel's re-straining hand kept him from pulling the stretcher out himself. He wanted to help, to do something other than stand by helplessly and watch. He didn't like being pushed aside. He didn't like the images hovering at the sidelines of his consciousness, taunting him.

"Josh, let them do their jobs."

Rachel's authoritative tone brought a halt to his chaotic mind. She was right. He was getting in the way. He stepped back and allowed the EMTs to do their job. They transferred Griff to a gurney and rushed toward the emergency room entrance.

He took Rachel's hand and followed the gurney into the hospital. An orderly moved forward, blocking the way. "Are you the boy's parents?"

"Yes." Josh looked past the man to where they'd wheeled Griff behind a curtain. "I need to be with my son."

"You can't go back there, sir. The doctors will take good care of your boy." The orderly gestured toward the administration desk. "If you could step over to the counter and fill out some standard forms…sir?"

Josh ignored the young man. He couldn't see his son, couldn't see what was happening. He pulled Rachel forward. "This is Dr. Maguire. She's my son's doctor. She needs to be with him."

The man frowned. "I thought you—"

Josh turned to Rachel and pleaded, "Please, go be with Griff. At least until I can call his pediatrician."

She stared up at him, her complexion a pasty white. Something akin to fear shifted in her gaze. Josh didn't understand. She was an E.R. doctor and he was asking her to do her job.

The young orderly puffed himself up. "Sir, she can't. She's not part of our staff."

Josh waited, ignoring the man's pronouncement. There was a struggle going on in Rachel. He could see the flicking emotions in her blue eyes. He didn't understand why she was hesitating.

Finally she blinked and straightened. Steely determination filled her gaze, crowding the fear to the edges. She focused on the orderly. "I'd like to speak to the attending."

The man frowned. "He's unavailable. You can leave a message—"

"I'd like to speak to him *now*," she demanded, her voice strong and cold.

The young man flushed and seemed to look around for help. "Uh, well. I—I think…"

Rachel started walking, her steps decisive. "Lead the way."

The man stared at her retreating back, speechless for a second, then hurried after her.

Josh could understand the orderly's reaction. Rachel's cool, commanding tone was formidable. Clearly she was a woman used to being in charge. There was a remarkable strength in her petite form. He took a deep breath and the tightness in his chest eased somewhat, secure in knowing she'd take care of his son, though the fear he'd seen in her eyes nagged at him. What was that about?

As each step forward drew Rachel closer to the place where her mother died, her spirit groaned in agony. She didn't want to do this, she'd stayed away from this place since that day, but now she had to walk in there. For Griff's sake.

She pursed her lips tightly. *Be honest with yourself, Rachel. This is for Josh.* Because he needed her to go in there. She couldn't explain how deeply his trust overwhelmed her and filled her with strength she'd not thought possible.

She approached the metal swinging doors leading to the restricted emergency care area and her steps faltered. A chill ran down her arms raising pinpricks of dread. Lifting her chin, she vowed to face the demons haunting her even if they destroyed her.

For Josh.

Josh was determined to do something, anything, to keep from rushing back to where they'd taken Griff. Nervous energy flowed through him as he moved to the administration desk. "What papers do you need filled out?"

The woman behind the desk smiled and handed him a clipboard and pen. "Here, sir. Fill in both sides, please."

Taking the clipboard, Josh sat in the waiting area and filled out the forms. He focused on the papers in front of him, fighting off the memories of the last time he'd been in the emergency room filling out similar forms.

As the minutes turned into what seemed like hours, a feeling of helplessness settled over him like a blanket of fog. Pacing the waiting room like a caged tiger didn't help. Nothing did. All he could do was wait. He hated to wait.

Rod, who had arrived shortly after Rachel disappeared with the orderly, sat in one of the stiff chairs, his legs stretched out in front of him. "Sit down, son. You're making me more nervous."

With an exasperated glance, Josh stopped and

stared out the window. His reflection looked back at him, accusingly.

Remembrance seeped in—memories and images of the night his wife had died. The gruesome reality of her death and his guilt struck at him, battering his already-weakened sense of self.

They'd brought her here to the emergency room; she'd undoubtedly disappeared down the hall on a gurney much the same way Griff had. She hadn't survived. He shuddered with the sense of loathing and uselessness that had plagued him for years. He couldn't change what had happened. No amount of penitence would bring her back.

He had to focus on Griff. That was the only thing that kept him sane, that kept him going. He had to be the best father he could be for Griff.

Abruptly he turned from the window and resumed pacing. It shouldn't take so long. Why hadn't Rachel come to tell him how Griff was?

"Josh." A dark-haired man with gentle brown eyes walked into the waiting area.

"Dr. Michaelson." Josh hurried over to Griff's pediatrician. Though the doctor was only a few years older than Josh, he exuded an aura of maturity and quiet compassion that appealed to Josh. Josh felt comforted by Dr. Michaelson's presence. "How is he?"

"He's awake and asking for you. Hi, Rod." The doctor acknowledged Rod, who came to stand beside them.

"Doc." Rod's good-natured reply elicited a smile from the doctor.

"And he's okay?" Josh asked, holding a breath.

"He'll have a nasty bruise and headache to match for a few days. We set his ankle in a cast, but it's a fairly minor break. He'll need to stay off his feet for a while, but other than that he's fine.'' Dr. Michaelson smiled.

Josh let out his breath. "Thank you, God."

Rod clapped Josh on the back. "Let's go see the little tiger."

Dr. Michaelson led the way to the elevators and stepped in with them. "He's been moved upstairs to a private room. He'll be released in the morning."

When the elevator doors closed, Josh stuck out his hand. "Thank you, Dr. Michaelson."

The doctor shook Josh's hand and gave a small chuckle. "You're welcome. Though I didn't do much. Dr. Maguire had everything under control when I arrived."

Josh breathed a grateful sigh of relief to know that Rachel had taken good care of his son.

The three men arrived at Griff's room and heard laughter. Josh stepped in, followed closely by Rod and Dr. Michaelson, to see his son smiling and chuckling at Rachel as she made funny faces while telling him a story.

"So you see—oh, here's your dad." Rachel hastily stood; a hesitant smile played at the corners of her mouth. She'd acquired a pair of green scrubs, which hugged her form attractively.

"Dad," Griff exclaimed, his eyes lighting up.

Josh rushed to his son's side and gave him a fierce hug. Overwhelmed by love and relief, his voice broke. "I'm so thankful you're okay."

Griff sniffed. "I'm sorry, Dad. I shouldn't have left the group."

"No, you shouldn't have. But we can talk about that later." He put his heart in his smile as he gazed with love at his boy. He was aware of Rachel as she walked around the bed and hugged Rod. Annoyed that she hadn't reacted that way with him, Josh said stiffly, "Thank you, Rachel, for everything."

She turned startled eyes on him. "You're welcome, Josh."

He held her gaze for a long moment, craving for her to show him the same affection she so easily doled out to the rest of his family. *Get a grip, man. You'll never be a priority in her life.* Chief of staff. That was her goal, not him.

He broke the eye contact because it was too painful to get lost in her winter-blue gaze.

He smoothed back a lock of Griff's hair that had fallen over the awful goose egg on his forehead. "Good thing you have such a tough noggin," he teased, trying to distract himself from the allure of Rachel's presence.

Behind him, he heard Rachel murmur something to his father and then she left along with Dr. Michaelson. Some of the energy in the room left with her and Josh sagged into a chair, acknowledging how much he'd depended on her today. That had to end here and now. She would leave in the morning. And with her she would take a piece of his heart, just as she'd done the first time she'd left.

All that had transpired in the past few hours hit Rachel with the force of a dump truck, and a quiver shook her bottom lip. She staggered to the wall.

She'd worked in the E.R. where her mother had died.

And she had survived.

Her mind was a jumbled, chaotic mess. And her emotions were riding a runaway roller coaster.

The first few moments after she'd walked through the swinging doors, choking memories had reared to life. But then she'd realized that nothing was as she remembered it. The tall doctor with the sad, brown eyes, who'd informed her that her mother was dead, wasn't there.

Logically she acknowledged he'd be past retirement age by now. But his face had haunted her nightmares.

But the biggest difference and the greatest healing came when she noticed that many of the triage techniques she'd implemented in her own hospital and others around the country had been duplicated at Sonora Community.

The attending had been more than gracious and overflowing with compliments as he'd explained how the papers she'd written and had published in popular medical journals over the past few years had changed the procedures of Sonora Community's E.R.

Tears welled in her eyes and a cleansing sob broke free as a huge weight was lifted from her chest. Her mother hadn't died in vain. Knowing that helped her to release the anger and bitterness she'd harbored toward the doctors and staff of the hospital.

And she wouldn't have ever had that confirmed if Josh hadn't asked her to stay with Griff. *Thank you, God, for using Griff and Josh to heal me.*

Josh's trust meant so much, yet his harsh words came floating back: *I have to protect him from you.*

He trusted her as a doctor but not as a woman. She supposed she should be thankful that at least he'd acknowledged her capabilities as a physician. There was a measure of comfort in his acknowledgment.

She shuddered as she recalled the panic and fear in his eyes out at the lake. When he'd first seen Griff lying there on the ground, she'd seen the flash of agony in his face and had known he'd thought for an instant that his son was dead. His relief was tangible.

His admission that he'd froze came as a surprise. Not that he'd recognized his reaction but that'd he'd admitted as much. She could only imagine what saying those words to her had cost him, showing any weakness to the person he'd accused of breaking his heart. Compassion and tenderness had welled up inside her. Josh was mature enough to expose his fallibility.

But when he'd taken her hand in the ambulance and held on as if she were his lifeline, her already tightly strung nerves nearly shattered, leaving her a bit dizzy with... She couldn't grasp what she'd felt in those moments.

Hunger for more, a certain amount of pride that he'd needed her, hope that maybe he could begin to accept her and her drive to make a difference. She didn't know which emotion was prominent or if they'd just bunched together into a single, unidentifiable glob.

Then he'd done something that had made even that jumbled-up mess of emotions pale in comparison. He'd said yes when asked if they were Griff's parents.

He couldn't possibly know the deep, soul-piercing pain he'd caused her.

The kicker had come when he'd entered the room after Griff had awakened. His very polite and indifferent thank-you had warred with the look in his eyes.

For a long, tense moment there'd been a yearning she hadn't seen in a very long time. An answering need had awakened in her, a longing to reach out to him and hold him close, only to be shot down as the look in his eyes shifted to something hostile and dangerous. As if he'd just remembered who and what she was. The woman he didn't want in his life, the woman he'd accused of breaking his heart. The woman he didn't love.

She'd have to remember that. He didn't love her. His heart mourned for his wife. Thinking him a wounded soul kept her from indulging in self-pity. She couldn't compete with a dead woman. She couldn't compete with his ideals. She didn't want to, she told herself sternly.

She'd made a promise and she intended to keep her side of the deal, for Griff's sake and to prove to Josh she could be a part of Griff's life without causing him irreparable damage. Through Griff she could take care of Josh and fulfill her promise to Mom G. That was the only way it was going to happen.

With that thought solidly established, Rachel headed for the one place that had always made her feel needed, the one place she could lose herself and calm her own frazzled nerves. She headed for the E.R. in hopes they could use some help.

Hours later, Rachel rolled her shoulders to relieve the tension in her bunched-up muscles. The clock on the E.R. wall read twelve-thirty in the morning. She slipped into the elevator, pushed the button for Griff's floor and leaned against the metal wall.

She'd been working for a long time and she was exhausted, but calmer. These hours spent doing what she'd been trained to do reminded her how much she loved her job, how much meaning her life held. And knowing that she'd conquered her demons lifted her spirits in a way she hadn't felt before.

The elevator opened and she exited. The dimly lit hall revealed a lone nurse sitting at the nurses' station. The woman smiled at Rachel. Rachel pointed down the hall. The nurse nodded and resumed whatever she'd been doing.

Rachel moved soundlessly to Griff's room. She wanted to check on him and make sure he slept comfortably. She was almost certain to find Josh in the room, as well, and she hoped he'd found some rest, too.

As she eased open the door, a muffled sound met her ears. She frowned and stepped into the room. Griff slept peacefully, his face young and innocent in repose. In the chair next to the bed sat Josh. His head was bowed and one of his hands held Griff's hand.

Josh was crying.

Chapter Thirteen

Tears streamed down Josh's cheeks and his breathing came shallow and fast. Immediately Rachel's gaze jumped back to Griff. Her heart pounded with dread until she saw the gentle rise and fall of his chest. She let out a relieved breath. He was sound asleep.

Her attention turned back to the big man sitting there weeping and her heart contracted painfully in her chest. She tried to reconcile this hurting man to the strong man who'd anchored her when her own torrent of tears threatened to sweep her away. The need to comfort, the need to help, propelled her forward. She reached his side and laid a hand gently on his shoulder. "Josh?"

He stiffened. The feel of him recoiling hurt, but she held her ground just as he had when she'd needed to grieve. She owed him this kindness and she stayed because her very essence wouldn't permit her to retreat. She was a healer; she couldn't walk away from someone in need.

Especially if that someone was Josh.

Rachel squeezed Josh's shoulder, the muscles beneath her palm rock hard and solid. He raised his head; the ragged expression on his strong, handsome face tore at her heart. He stared straight ahead.

"What are you doing here?" His lowered voice rang with harshness.

"I came to check on you both."

"We're fine."

Right. "It shows."

He flinched and wiped his eyes with the back of his free hand.

"Josh, what's wrong?"

A long silent moment passed. He was fighting to stay in control. She understood what that was like, the energy and the concentration it took to keep from being vulnerable to the emotions that threatened to overwhelm and destroy. She took a deep breath, wanting to help, to take away whatever it was that was eating at him, even if he didn't want her to. "Remember what you said to me?"

He didn't respond.

She kneeled next to the chair and turned his face toward her with her hand, his stubbled jaw prickly to her touch. His tortured eyes, looking bleak and lost, ripped at her soul. She had to help him.

"'You have to let it out or it will eat away at you.'" She quoted the words he'd spoken to her that day when she'd cried in his arms. "Josh, whatever it is, you can tell me."

"I can't. You don't want to know."

The suffering in his voice brought fresh tears to clog her throat. She laid her hand on his cheek, her thumb gently caressing.

His eyes closed briefly, accepting her offer of solace. Satisfaction flowed through her. Empathy for his
pain tightened her chest. Such a strange mix of emotions.

He pulled away. "I don't deserve your comfort or
your concern."

The utter lack of emotion in his hushed voice sent
a shiver down her spine and started the reconstruction
of the wall around her heart. She withdrew her hand,
stung that even now he would push her away. At least
she'd tried. "Don't deserve or don't want?"

"There's no absolution for what I've done."

The self-recriminations in his tone made her shake
her head. "Griff's accident was not your fault. He's
going to be okay."

He gave a short, humorless laugh. "I know that.
Griff's the only thing I've done right in my life."

His cryptic remarks confused her. "That's not true.
You help people every day doing your job."

He shot her a sharp glance. "Yeah, well. A career
doesn't make up for a lost life."

"A lost life…" Realization dawned. "Andrea."

His gaze grew distant; his body drew inward, closing Rachel out. She'd known Josh mourned his wife,
but she hadn't really understood how deep his grief
went.

"You must have loved her a great deal," she whispered past the lump in her throat.

She didn't know what to say to ease his pain. Or
her own. Behind her wall of defense, the tiny corner
of her heart that held the dream of Josh's love with-
ered. Even if she could stay longer than she intended,
she didn't stand a chance against the memory of the
love he and Andrea had shared.

He glanced at Griff, then gave a sharp negative shake of his head before abruptly standing and moving by the window.

Rachel rose. Her heart hammered in her chest. What had he meant? That he hadn't loved Andrea or that he wasn't going to talk to Rachel about his wife? She watched him for a long, tense moment. His rigid stance screamed isolation, but the agony marring his handsome features belied his body language.

She'd promised Mom G. she'd take care of Josh. She'd wanted to fulfill the promise through Griff. But she needed to reach out to Josh. He'd unknowingly helped heal her scarred soul. It was her turn to help him.

Grim determination straightened her spine. She didn't want Griff to wake up and see his father so distressed. She closed the distance between them and laid a hand on Josh's arm.

He looked down at her hand, then met her gaze. She sucked in a breath at the torment in his eyes. "For Griff's sake, please let me help."

His jaw tightened.

"Stubborn man," she muttered with frustration.

The corner of his mouth quirked up, reminding her of when he'd said the same thing about her. Rachel narrowed his gaze on him as an idea formed. He'd wrapped her in his arms and had refused to let go when he'd said those words.

Not taking the time to rationalize why what she was about to do was dangerous to her heart, she stepped closer and slipped her arms around his waist. His breath hitched and she tightened her hold.

"Rachel," he groaned, his tone full of warning and longing.

"It's okay. Everything will be okay," she said into his shirt.

"No." His hands came down on her shoulders and tried gently to push her away. She refused to budge.

"Everything will never be okay," he stated in a shattered voice.

"Why?"

He stopped pushing. She leaned back to look up at him. "Why, Josh? Why won't everything be okay?"

"You don't want to know." His hands dropped away from her and he shifted within the confines of her loosened hold.

Suddenly, holding him seemed awkward and inappropriate. She stepped back and let her arms fall to her side. "Tell me."

A noise broke from him. Agonizing to hear, full of misery and torture. He didn't answer. He walked to Griff's bedside and stared down at his son. Rachel was almost relieved that he wanted to back away from the heartache of his story, but she could see the suffering in his eyes.

She walked to stand beside him.

He sighed. "You're not going to let this lie, are you?"

"No," she said softly.

He ran a finger down Griff's cheek. "I love him, you know. More than I love my own life."

"I know." She slipped her hand into his, wanting to share her strength. "Let's take a walk so we don't disturb him."

Josh swallowed and then nodded. They left the room and walked down the corridor. She wasn't sure where to go, but then she realized that Josh had taken the lead. He led them to the hospital chapel. The softly lit sanctuary was empty. They slid into the back pew.

"Tell me what's eating at you," she gently prodded.

His gaze shifted from her face to the stained glass window. The misery so clear in his expression tore at her heart. She didn't know what memory was playing behind his glazed, wide-eyed stare, but whatever images he saw were harrowing. His pain made her ache in a way she never had before. *Lord, give me strength to help him.*

He closed his eyes, and a violent shudder wracked his body. When he opened his eyes and turned to stare down at her, she drew back at the blank, desolate look.

"I killed my wife."

Shock reverberated through Rachel. He wasn't serious. He couldn't be. He was only trying to scare her, drive her away. Josh would never kill anyone. She was as sure of that as she was that God loved her and had a plan for her life. Neither belief was tangible, but true just the same.

"Were you driving the car?" she asked, prepared for his answer to be yes.

"No."

She blinked. "But Mom G. said she'd died in a car accident."

"She did."

Those two words left her more confused. "Then how can you be responsible?"

"Because," he responded fiercely, "she was in that car because of me."

She frowned. That was so like a guy to not come out with a straight answer. She contemplated him a moment. Her instincts told her he wouldn't respond to her coddling him, but he would respond to logical and rational reasoning.

Succeeding in a male-dominated profession had taught her to draw her male counterparts out with challenging questions delivered unemotionally. The men in her world wouldn't tolerate an emotional female. She schooled her features into impassivity and said, "But it was an accident, right? How can you be at fault?"

"We'd argued."

For Josh's marriage to be suddenly cut short in the midst of an argument was undoubtedly a hard blow.

"I should've stopped her. I shouldn't have let her get in the car. I should've never kept…" His voice trailed off and he suddenly looked angry.

"That's a lot of *should have*s," Rachel stated quietly. "Did you somehow become omnipotent? Do you believe you could have stopped something out of your control?"

His scathing look was razor sharp. "It wasn't out of my control."

"How could you control an accident?"

"It wasn't just an accident, Rachel. It was so much worse." He turned back toward the window and fisted his hands. "So much worse."

Frustrated with him and aching for him all at the same time, she touched his arm. "Tell me what happened."

"That night I was working late, a double shift. Something I'd been doing a lot then. The nanny called. Said Andrea had locked herself in the bedroom and she could hear things crashing."

He shook his head as if trying to deny what he was

remembering. "I had to break down the bedroom door. She had torn the place apart. I was...shocked. She threw shoes at me and punched me. I grabbed her and shook her, demanding to know why she was behaving like a lunatic."

He closed his eyes, and she could only guess at the images in his mind. "She'd been crying. Her eyes were swollen and red, her cheeks stained with her tears. She jerked out of my grasp, screaming at me."

"Oh, Josh," Rachel whispered, her chest tightening with anguish for him. "Why was she so angry?"

The misery etching lines in his face made her want to hold him. "She'd found a picture I'd hidden away."

"A picture?"

With extreme effort she refrained from flinching at the guilt and self-loathing emanating from his eyes.

"The picture of us by our tree," he said, his voice painful to listen to, the tone ravaged and scarred.

Then the meaning in his words hit Rachel full force and the breath left her body in a rush. He'd saved something of *their* past together. She knew which picture he meant. *The picture of us by our tree.* The tree where they'd found Griff. The tree Josh had carved their initials in, surrounded by a heart.

The week before she'd left for college, they'd driven up to the lake wanting to spend as much time together as possible. Those last few weeks were tense because Josh had been hurt by her refusal of his marriage proposal. That day had been no different.

The entire drive to the lake, they'd fought about her need to become a doctor. He wouldn't compromise. She'd tried to tell him of her mother's death and the effect it had had on her, but he hadn't wanted to hear.

Finally, in desperation, she'd asked if they could spend a few hours together without thinking about anything but the here and now. And they had. For a few short hours no one else existed. Only their love mattered.

They'd propped the camera on a rock and used the timer to record the moment. But as dusk came, so had reality. They'd driven home in silence, the tension returning. One week later she'd left.

Josh had hidden away that picture. She didn't understand, couldn't begin to make sense of this.

And Andrea... Rachel imagined the pain Andrea had felt, the jealousy she'd experienced when she found her husband had saved a memento of his ex-girlfriend. A sick feeling moved through her. "She drove off in a rage?"

He nodded. The deep grooves around his eyes showed the strain of loss.

"You can't take responsibility for that."

"It was my fault," he insisted.

Hurting for him and Griff, she tried to make him see reason. "She was a grown woman. She made the choice to drive while upset. That's not your fault." Rachel could see the disbelief in the depths of his hazel eyes.

"You don't understand, Rachel. She wrapped her car around that tree on purpose." He shuddered as if haunted by the memory. "I saw the finality in her eyes as she tore out of the driveway."

Her mind recoiled from accepting that thought. "You don't know that as fact. Why didn't you tell her the picture didn't mean anything?"

He closed his eyes. His mouth tightened into a grim line as if somehow he could stop the words from coming. She'd pushed him this far; she wasn't going to let him back away from letting out whatever was destroying him inside.

Even as her hand reached for him, she acknowledged that in touching him, she felt connected to him in a way she'd never felt with anyone else.

She rubbed his arm until his hand captured hers. Fascinated, she watched as he brought her palm to his lips. He kissed the tender flesh, then slid his lips to her fingertips before replacing her hand in her lap. She shivered with the impact of those gentle kisses.

"You didn't answer my question," she stated, her voice shaky.

When he looked at her, the tenderness swirling in the hazel depths of his eyes sent her heart racing. When he spoke, his words made her breathing screech to a halt.

"Because it would've been a lie."

Josh waited for Rachel to say something, anything. Instead, he watched the coldness come over her, seeping into her glacier-blue gaze. The doctor was back.

"Well, I can certainly understand how that would've made your wife more unhappy," she said dryly.

He blinked.

A little crease appeared between her dark brows. "That still doesn't give you the right to own all the guilt for Andrea's death."

"What do you mean? Of course I'm guilty. She wouldn't have been in the car if she hadn't found that picture I'd kept and she wouldn't have driven away if I'd stopped her. If I'd been a better husband, none of this would have happened. If I'd loved her enough. Been enough...'' The words broke from him in an anguished rush.

She shook her head. "Wow, I thought doctors were the only ones susceptible to God complexes."

He rubbed his face wearily. "When did you develop such a biting wit?"

"Josh, listen to me." Her authoritative tone demanded attention. "I have no doubt you were a good husband. But you're right, Josh, you weren't enough."

Shocked, the air left his body as if he'd been pushed off a cliff and was free-falling without a parachute.

Josh looked into her eyes, expecting to see condemnation but instead saw cool compassion.

"Only God's enough. And you aren't God. He gives each of us free will. Andrea could have chosen to handle the situation differently. Unfortunately, you have to live with the results of her choice." Her gaze shifted away. "We all have to live with the results of others' choices and...our own. Some good, some bad. Some necessary, others optional."

The wisdom in her words touched him deeply. Did she regret the choices she'd made? "You're an amazing woman, Rachel Maguire."

She raised a brow at him, a joking glint in her blue eyes. "You're just now figuring that out?"

"I've always known. I'm just starting to appreciate it more." And it was true. He did appreciate her strength, her compassion and her wit.

A faint tinge of pink brightened her cheeks but the look in her eyes turned impossibly colder before she quickly checked her watch. "It's, uh, late. Or early, depending on your frame of reference. You—you should check on Griff. Yes, that's what you should do.'' She stood, her spine rigid and straight.

Was she flustered? She rambled as if she was, but her body language said otherwise. He'd like to be able to figure her out. But he would never get the chance.

Slowly he stood. ''And you have a plane to catch.''

A hollow feeling settled in the pit of his stomach. He hated the thought of her leaving, of never seeing her again, but he knew it was for the best. His heart couldn't take much more damage.

''Oh, yes. I do have to take care of my flight.'' She walked out of the chapel and to the elevators.

Josh followed. His heart twisted in his chest at her cold and unemotional acknowledgment of her departure.

Once they were inside the elevator, she pushed the button for Griff's floor and then the lobby.

Josh frowned. ''You're not coming to see Griff?''

She didn't look at him. ''I need to use the phone. Dr. Hunford, the E.R. attending, said I could use the doctor's lounge in the E.R.''

''You could use the phone in Griff's room.''

She glanced at him. ''I don't want to disturb him.''

''Griff will be upset if he doesn't get to see you before you leave.'' Just thinking about having to tell his son she'd left for good made his stomach churn.

She turned her crystal gaze on him and cocked her head speculatively. ''What about your request that I stay away from him?''

Josh ran a hand through his hair. ''I overreacted. I shouldn't have said that.''

''No, you shouldn't have.'' Her expression softened slightly. ''But I understand.''

He touched her cheek, enjoying the softness of her skin beneath his callused hand. "Do you?" he asked quietly, wondering if she really understood she had the power to destroy all of their hearts.

She swallowed. His eyes were drawn to the slender column of her neck, to the visible pulse point in her creamy skin. He leaned toward her with every intention of kissing her.

Then the elevator doors opened.

Rachel stepped back, her eyes wide and cool.

Reining in his attraction, he asked, "We'll see you later?"

She nodded and the elevator doors slid shut, leaving Josh to deal with the sad ache gripping his heart. Resignation lay heavy on his shoulders. She'd leave and he's miss her.

Again.

Chapter Fourteen

As soon as the doors closed and she was alone in the elevator, Rachel slumped against the cool surface of the wall. Josh had almost kissed her. And she'd have let him. She wanted him to, actually.

Josh and his son had demolished the barricade she'd placed around her heart. She felt beat-up and bruised. But recuperation would have to wait until she returned to Chicago. Which meant if she were truly committed to staying a few more days, she'd have to shore up her defenses and guard her heart and her emotions like a fortress.

But not tonight. She ached too much to do anything. Everything Josh had revealed left her reeling.

Andrea's tragic death made Rachel's insides quiver with sadness and guilt.

Sadness for what Josh had lost—his wife, his complete family and his dream. Sadness for Griff who lost his mother before he ever got a chance to know her.

Guilt. No, she wouldn't own the guilt. It was not

her fault that Andrea drove into that tree. Nor was it Josh's, regardless of what he believed.

The man was too honorable, too generous and caring to be burdened with such guilt. She wanted to protect him, to make his life better. These feelings were so different, so much more than what she'd felt for him in high school. More intense, deeper. Based not on the fantasies of a starry-eyed teenager but on the reality of loving the man Josh had become.

The admission made her already-weak knees tremble as the elevator door slid open. Placing one foot in front of the other and walking out into the hall took a great deal of concentration.

She loved Josh.

Not with a girl's infatuation but with a grown woman's love. And not only with a tiny corner of her heart, but with the whole kit and caboodle. Every defense she had crumbled to smithereens, laying her heart and emotions exposed and vulnerable.

Lord, what do I do now?

Telling him served no purpose. Her life was in Chicago, his here in Sonora.

But thinking about the small apartment she called home filled her with emptiness. Even thinking about Cook County Hospital, her prestigious position and the tremendous accomplishments in triage care, working to prevent a repeat of her mother's experience, didn't fill the vacant spots. Only thoughts of Josh, Griff and the big Victorian house caused warmth to spread through her and pushed away the empty coldness.

She entered the deserted lounge and put her hand on the phone. She'd thought the decision to stay was for Griff's sake, but the decision had been for Josh and herself, as well. He needed her even if he didn't know it.

And she needed him.

She'd never realized how much until now.

She'd thought she was getting along fine in life alone, when in actuality she'd had Mom G. as a safety net. Now that she was in reality alone, with no family, she didn't want to be alone.

She wanted more. Mom G. had said God wanted more for her. More than a career. She couldn't discount the satisfaction that came from her work, but the long lonely years ahead stretched out before her, making her want to find the *more* that God had waiting for her.

She hoped it was Josh. She needed his steady presence, his solid strength. She needed his force of character, honest and fair, though at times misguided in his attempts to protect himself and those he loved. Could he love her? The question bounced around her head and her pulse sped up.

Then another thought came slamming home. She could live in Sonora and still practice medicine because the hospital no longer held the haunting specter of her mother's unnecessary death. Her mother hadn't died in vain. Rachel had made a difference and could continue on in this hospital.

With her heart beating in her throat, she quickly made her calls, leaving her return to Chicago open-ended.

She would stay and see if there was any hope for her and Josh. She prayed that this was part of God's plan because it was now part of hers.

Josh stepped out of the elevator and into the E.R. People milled through the waiting area and he felt a pang of sympathy. He remembered all too well what it was like waiting to find out if your life would ever be the same again. He suppressed the shudder that rippled over him and searched for the doctors' lounge.

Not seeing any marked doors, he headed toward a man in a white coat. The name tag on the man's breast pocket identified him as Dr. Hunford. He remembered Rachel mentioning him. "Excuse me, Doctor. Could you point me toward the doctors' lounge?"

Bushy black brows rose over dark eyes. "Can I help you with something?"

Josh smiled politely. "I'm looking for a friend who was going to use the lounge phone."

Dr. Hunford returned his smile. "You mean Dr. Maguire?"

"Have you seen her?"

"Come with me."

Dr. Hunford led the way down a hallway. "Do you know Dr. Maguire well?"

He answered, "Yes."

Did he know her well? Josh considered the question. He knew many things about Rachel. She was generous with her time, affectionate and loving toward his son, full of compassion and strength, a competent doctor, authoritative and challenging until he thought he'd howl with frustration, and yet, she remained a mystery to him. The thoughts that accompanied those sparkling blue eyes, eyes that at times turned to cold ice, were hidden from him.

"It was a good thing for us that Dr. Maguire has a license to practice in the state of California. We were in quite a pickle last night with the pileup on

Highway 108. We appreciated all her help,'' Dr. Hunford said.

Josh frowned. She'd helped in the E.R. last night? When he'd thought she'd gone back to her hotel, she'd been down here. She must be exhausted.

As they approached a room marked Doctors' Lounge, Rachel stepped out. She smiled when she saw the two men. Josh sucked in a breath. She hadn't smiled like that since... He couldn't remember seeing her smile with that much warmth since she'd returned. At least not at him. His son received smiles like that but Josh didn't. He narrowed his eyes. He didn't get it. What did she have up her sleeve?

"Here she is," Dr. Hunford said unnecessarily.

"Dr. Hunford, Joshua. You were looking for me?" she said, her tone cheery.

Josh's suspicions deepened. She never called him Joshua. He thought back through the years. The only time he could recall her using the formal form of his name was... His eyes widened and his gaze jumped to her face.

When they'd been at their tree. She'd wanted to stop fighting and had distracted him with his name on her lips and that glorious mouth drove all arguments from his head.

What was going on?

Dr. Hunford smiled. "I wanted to say thank you for pitching in last night."

"You're welcome. I enjoyed working alongside your staff. They're very good."

Dr. Hunford puffed with pride. "They are. But we could sure use more people like you around here. Any chance you'll be sticking around?"

The subtle glance the man gave Josh was rife with

meaning. Josh suppressed the urge to roll his eyes and say, "Yeah, when gold flows freely through the Mother Lode again."

Her smile faltered slightly. "I'll be in town for at least a few more days."

Okay. As announcements went, it was like a good sock in the stomach. His brows rose as wariness twisted in his chest. What sweet torture was she planning now? "You will?"

She tugged on her bottom lip. The subtle sign of uncertainty rocked Josh. Even when she'd broken down, she hadn't been unsure of herself. Dr. Hunford's gaze bobbed between Josh and Rachel with great interest. Josh wished the man would go away.

"Because…ummm…Griff." Her gaze slid away and then back again. Gone was the hesitancy. Cold determination filled her eyes and her chin went up. "Because you need me to help out with Griff."

Josh gaped at her. "Excuse me?"

Rachel smiled patiently. "Griff's being released today and you still have a fire to deal with."

Oh, man. Rachel staying to help him would only prolong the agony for him and Griff. "I've got my dad."

She arched a black brow. "Your dad has already gone to help with the fire."

He narrowed his gaze. "I'll manage. We've done perfectly well for years without you." He threw her words back at her, not caring that Dr. Hunford was really interested now.

He felt the pierce of her narrowed gaze. "You always had Mom G. to help. Now you have me."

Anger flared hot. Until she got bored and decided

the hospital was where she'd rather be. "I don't need you."

Dr. Hunford chose that moment to interrupt. "Well, I do."

Josh swung his angry gaze to the doctor, who blinked owlishly.

Rachel smiled that annoying polite, professional smile. "I'll let you know if I have time to help out."

Dr. Hunford began to back up. "Wonderful. We're shorthanded for the next week or so and I'd love the opportunity to discuss your innovative techniques I've read so much about." He disappeared around the corner.

A week or so. Josh fumed. She would not be staying a week or so. He couldn't take having her in town any longer, not when all he wanted to do was kiss that calm-and-collected look off her beautiful face. He fisted his hands. "You are not staying."

"Yes, I am."

"Why?"

Her smile never changed. "I told you why. You have a fire to deal with. I'm staying until you put it out."

He didn't know if he'd ever be able to put out the fire she'd ignited in his blood. He'd seen the damage a fire could cause. He didn't intend to get burned. Again. "I'll figure something out. Leave as planned."

She shrugged. "I've already changed my plans."

"Unchange them."

"No." The stubborn tilt to her chin didn't bode well. "You're wasting time. Let's get Griff home."

He gritted his teeth. There had to be another way. He could call Jen and see if she'd take care of Griff. No, he couldn't add to her already-busy life. Griff was going to need a lot of attention at first. Josh would tell his father to go home. That's what he'd do.

"Josh, the fire."

"All right, all right," he said, irritated by her reminder. What choice did he have? He would have to allow her to come to the house and stay with Griff until he could send Dad home from the fire. And then he'd send Rachel packing, boxing up his hopes and wishes to be shipped along with her.

Josh pulled the truck to a halt in front of his house. Fury churned and twisted in his chest, mingling with worry. His father had refused to leave the station and return home to relieve Rachel of her charge. In fact, his father had elected to sleep at the station. Rod's misguided attempts at matchmaking were wearing thin.

To make matters worse, the blaze had jumped the fire line.

Josh hadn't been able to even think about going home until well past dark, which left his son with Rachel for hours. Oh, he knew she'd take good care of him. Too good of care. She'd be affectionate and funny with Griff. She probably had tons of stories to tell and would make his son's heart swell with love. Which would make her leaving that much harder.

He opened the front door. The house was quiet. A single light from the family room lent its glow to guide him. He stopped inside the doorway, his breath trapped somewhere between his lungs and his heart.

Rachel sat on the couch. She'd changed from the green scrubs into—he blinked, stunned—his sweat suit.

Her eyes were closed, dark lashes rested against her

milky complexion and her lustrous hair spread across the cushions. Her crossed ankles were propped up on the coffee table. He dragged his eyes away from her red-tipped toes to Griff. His small, round head rested on Rachel's lap and his broken ankle lay resting on another pillow.

Bittersweet longing hit him square between the eyes. If only this scene were real. He longed for Rachel to be his wife, for her to be his son's mother. He longed to come home from work like this and see her here waiting for him. To hear her voice filling the house with love and laughter. He longed for nights spent in her arms and to awaken in the morning light with her beside him.

He longed for a life that would never be.

She would never be content to be his wife. To live a simple life. To live again in this small town when the big city beckoned her away with excitement, when the hospital she worked at provided her the fulfillment she craved: a high-powered position with upward career possibilities. He couldn't compete with what she believed God had planned for her.

Just as he and his father hadn't been able to compete with the life his mother had wanted.

He must never forget that the most important thing to Rachel would always be her career. He hadn't been enough then, and he wouldn't be now.

And the quicker he got her out of his house the better. So Griff wouldn't be hurt like he'd been hurt.

But what was he to do with her tonight? He couldn't leave Griff to take her to the hotel and he couldn't leave her on the couch. She'd have to sleep in the guest room upstairs. Down the hall from his room.

He gulped.

Taking a deep breath, he moved to the couch and gingerly lifted Griff from her lap and carried him upstairs, careful of his ankle. Once his son was settled, Josh went to the guest room and turned down the bed.

He ignored the hammering in his chest at the thought of her beautiful dark hair spilling across the white pillow. He quickly spun away from the choking image.

Back downstairs, he contemplated how best to move Rachel upstairs. He rapidly dismissed the idea of waking her because facing a sleepy and cute Rachel was something he'd rather not do.

Cautiously he slipped a hand under her head and the other under her knees. He slowly lifted her, testing her weight. She barely weighed anything. Easily he raised her up in his arms and held her to him. She stirred, sighing slightly.

''Shh, its okay,'' he whispered.

Her arms slid around his neck and she nuzzled closer, her cheek warm against his chest. She'd showered, and the scent of Griff's shampoo clung to her soft hair. He'd never considered the smell of green apples an aphrodisiac.

Thinking himself insane for putting himself through such torture, he hurried upstairs with her. By the light of the moon coming through the window he laid her down gently on the soft bed and rested her head on the pillow. Her arms tightened around his neck and she made a soft sound of protest deep in her throat as he tried to extract himself.

He leaned in a little, his face close to hers, her arms allowing some slack. Her breath teased the hair at his temple. He closed his eyes against the zing of pleasure ricocheting through his veins and crippling his heart.

Every instinct urged him to gather her close and give in to the feminine allure of Rachel. To abandon all thought, all conscience and reasoning, for one precious moment in her arms.

God help me.

By strength drawn only from his faith, Josh gently pried her arms lose and laid them beside her. She snuggled into the bed and turned on her side. He swallowed and quickly pulled up the lightweight blanket, covering her slender curves.

He backed out of the room, very much aware that Rachel Maguire slept in his house. He doubted he'd get any sleep tonight.

Rachel bolted upright. She blinked, her eyes adjusting to the darkness broken slightly by the moonlight seeping through the crack of the curtain. She was in an unfamiliar room in a strange bed. Then it hit her. She smiled with pleasure. She was in Josh's house, apparently in the guest room.

She pushed the button on her watch and the circular dial lit up with a green glow. Two-forty in the morning.

The last thing she remembered was sitting on the couch with Griff, telling him the funnier stories from the E.R. The time was precious and she'd never felt so wanted or so satisfied. She belonged here with this family. Griff had finally dozed off and she must have, as well.

Tugging on the too-big sweatshirt she'd confiscated from Josh's dryer, pleasure welled up at the thought of Josh carrying her upstairs. With the way he'd reacted when she'd stated she was staying, it was little wonder he hadn't carted her back to the hotel. But he hadn't. He'd made her comfortable. He'd taken care of her. She liked the idea of Josh caring for her.

Yawning sleepily, she slid her feet off the bed and onto the floor. She stood, swaying slightly as blood rushed to her head. When her equilibrium returned, she shuffled to the door and peeked into the dark hall. She bit her lip trying to remember which way to the bathroom. She shrugged and started out to her left. Her big toe connected with something hard and solid which in turn connected with the wall.

"Ouch," she muttered at the small table, and steadied it with her hands, hoping the noise from the table scraping the wall hadn't disturbed anyone.

She tried the first door she came to, peering in. Griff's room. Pale moonlight shone on the sleeping boy. Rachel stood watching Griff sleep for a moment. He'd become so dear to her. Quietly she closed the door.

She turned to head the other way and ran into a big, firm mass. A small yelp escaped her.

"You okay?" Josh's groggy voice swept over her in the darkness, chasing away the last vestiges of sleep.

"Josh, you scared me," she whispered back.

"Sorry. Heard a noise. Wanted to make sure you were okay."

His sleep-husky voice sent a thrill down her spine. He was worried about her. "Just looking for the bathroom."

"Over here." His hand reached out and found her shoulder. Bits of fire raced along her arm and she trembled under the onslaught of emotions the heat sparked.

He guided her toward another door, opened it, flipped the switch and stepped back.

Rachel blinked in the sudden light. When she was able to focus, her heart twisted with tenderness. Josh looked so adorable standing there in his plaid flannel boxers and T-shirt, his hair mussed from sleep, his eyes drowsy and his expression unguarded. "Thank you for letting me sleep here tonight."

He smiled a sweet, boyish smile that melted her heart. "Anytime." He stepped forward and placed a feather-light kiss on her lips. "G'night." He turned and shuffled down the dark hall.

Rachel's breath caught and held as she watched him disappear into a room. The gentle caress seared her, branded her as his.

But would he ever claim her?

Chapter Fifteen

Her fingertips traced the warmth still lingering on her lips. He'd kissed her. Not a passionate, "I want you" kind of kiss, but a sweet, loving gesture that said "I care." The poignant moment stretched as she considered the implications of that single little kiss.

He cared. Whether he wanted to admit it or not, he cared. And if he cared, then love could follow. Not the same love from their teenage years. They were adults now. Different than they'd been back then. And their love would be different. If he could love her. Her heart pounded loudly in her ears.

If they loved each other enough, surely they could find a way to make their lives come together. A nagging feeling that tried to rob her of the hope of happiness warned that love hadn't been enough once.

She wouldn't let doubt interfere. So much had happened, changed. She'd changed. She would find a way to make this work. She held her breath.

Maybe they were being given another chance.

Oh, God. Please, please. I want Josh to see that I can be a wife, a mother and *a doctor.*

In the morning, Josh showered and dressed quickly. He checked on Griff who still slept soundly. He paused outside of the guest room door. He considered waking Rachel up and asking her to leave, but decided a note would do just as well. After his fitful night's sleep, he didn't think seeing her before he left would be a good thing. He'd dreamed way too much last night. And all of his dreams had centered on Rachel.

Quietly he went down the stairs. He headed for the kitchen, but a movement in his peripheral vision stopped him in his tracks. He turned slowly, his whole body becoming alert to Rachel's presence, but when he actually saw her, he wasn't prepared for the sight.

Stunned pleasure surged through his veins and his mind screamed what his heart wanted to deny. She shouldn't be wearing his old football jersey, the hem flirting with her knees. She shouldn't be moving so gracefully, her lithe slender body flowing through controlled movements. She shouldn't be in his house at all.

He couldn't tear his gaze away. Somewhere in his foggy brain he recalled knowing the type of martial art she was practicing, but he couldn't think, let alone come up with the name.

Her fluid movements took her through a complete range of motion. Her capable hands, rigid and taut, slid through the air. Her legs gently carried her petite form in a wide arc, yet her feet barely left the ground.

"Good morning, Josh."

Even her voice flowed, graceful and calm. A shiver

sent him into action. Averting his gaze, he began to pace, his heavy boots ringing hollow on the hardwood floor.

"You shouldn't be here," he said.

"Yes, I should," she replied firmly.

He shook his head. "No. When Griff wakes, you should go."

"You have a fire to put out, don't you?"

"The others can handle it."

He hated contemplating not going to the station, but he hated having her entrenched in his house even more because it was only temporary. He didn't want temporary.

He wanted forever.

She smoothly turned to face him, her hands competently cutting the air in front of her. "You'd hate that, Josh."

He stopped pacing and narrowed his gaze on her. "You think you know me so well, do you?"

A slight curving of her lips was her only answer.

"Rachel, I can't have you here anymore." He winced at the almost-desperate note in his voice. He ached all over, from his heart to his toes.

"Sure you can. You need me." She bent low at the knees, the hem of his old jersey riding up slightly to reveal firm muscle and curves. All the blood left his head.

"I don't need you," he said from between clenched teeth. He wanted her in the most base of ways but he did not need her. No way.

"Sure you do." She rose and rocked back on one heel. "You need me to stay with Griff."

"You're killing me here, Rachel," he choked out,

and tried to pry his gaze from where his jersey pulled tight across her shoulders.

She paused midmotion. A graceful statue, a work of art. A feminine smile curved her lips. He couldn't imagine her cold or distant at the moment. She glanced at him knowingly.

He was surprised he didn't just vaporize on the spot. "Rachel."

"You didn't have a problem with me being here last night." She moved again, a slow sweeping arc from left to right, her hands twisting through space.

"I didn't have a choice last night. You fell asleep." He certainly had a choice now. But his resolve to make her leave was rapidly slipping and being filled with impossible thoughts. Thoughts about how nice it was to find her here, wearing his shirt. To have her in his house, willing to take care of his son.

"You said I could stay anytime."

He frowned. "I did?"

"You don't remember?"

"Well...I vaguely remember getting up in the night. But I don't remember what I said." He'd been concerned when he'd heard her bang into the hall table.

"Or what you did?"

He rocked back on the heels of his boots. "Did?"

She pulled her limbs together and executed a neat bow. When she straightened, a smile as bright as lightning lit her face. "You kissed me."

He blinked, stunned by her smile. Stunned by her statement. He searched his memory; a fuzzy image of Rachel standing in the soft light flowing into the hall came to mind. He'd kissed her good-night. "I did." He swallowed. That simple little kiss changed nothing. She still had to leave. Quickly. Before he got ideas about more kisses. "I'll wake Griff. We'll take you to your hotel."

"I've already arranged for the hotel to messenger my things over."

"Rachel."

"Josh."

He balled his hands into fists. "Why are you doing this? I thought you wanted to get back to your precious hospital and your big-city life as quickly as you could."

She cocked her head to one side, her smile still in place, only a little less sunny. "We made a promise and I intend on keeping it. Right now, you need help with Griff."

"I'll take him with me."

She rolled her eyes and walked toward him, her bare feet small and graceful. His jersey swished against her knees. She laid a hand on his arm. "Let me do this. Please."

He shouldn't. He should make her leave. But with those big, crystal-blue eyes staring up at him so imploringly, so…warm, he couldn't resist. He couldn't resist the pull she had on him. His poor battered heart sunk. "For Griff you can stay."

She patted his arm. "Good. Now off with you. You have a job to do."

He glanced up the stairs. "Do you want me to carry Griff down for you?"

"Don't worry. We'll manage."

Yes, but would *he* manage? Josh worried he was making a mistake. He worried that his son would be hurt, that his own heart would not survive the next few days.

He worried he was losing his mind to allow her to stay. But she was right; he couldn't take Griff with him. He rationalized that another day couldn't cause any more damage than had already been done. So he allowed her to bustle him out the door. He'd deal with how to get her out of his life and his heart later. There was always later.

Rachel finished cleaning up the last of the mess she'd made while fixing dinner. The dark cabinets and gray speckled counters were wiped clean. The round kitchen dining table was set with four places. Fresh flowers in a jar added a sparkle to the room.

The aromas of warmed garlic bread and baked chicken with carrots and onions tempted her appetite. Where was Josh?

When he'd called earlier to check on Griff, he'd said he would be home around now. And when she'd said dinner would be ready and waiting for them, he'd sounded…put out. As if he didn't like the idea of her cooking. Did he think she couldn't handle the meal alone?

She chuckled. She'd put together a fancy feast. In fact, she'd found the domestic task shockingly pleasant. She would prove to Josh that she was not only skilled in healing but in the domestic arts, as well.

The whole day had been pleasant. She and Griff had watched a movie, he'd taught her how to play chess and she'd taught him how to play solitaire. They'd laughed and talked about sports, school and dreams.

Her maternal instincts that had kicked in days before were blooming full force, and she found this form of caretaking appealing.

As a doctor she was responsible to care for bodily injuries, but not emotional well-being. Fix 'Em And Move 'Em Out was the motto of the E.R. She'd always thought that was best for her. No attachments, no hassles. No risking of her heart. Always staying focused on making sure her mother hadn't died in vain. Her heart soared to know that she'd accomplished what she'd set out to do.

Now she was free to take the risk with Griff. And she was willing to take the risk with Josh, too. She'd come a long way in a short time. She smiled and glanced upward. *Is this part of Your plan, God?* She hoped her assumption was on target. There had to be a way to make Josh see that she could be a part of their lives.

The back door opened, startling her. She whirled around as Josh stepped through the doorway. He filled the frame; his towering presence made the air crackle with enflamed energy.

She loved to see him in his uniform. Loved the way the fabric hugged his muscles and the muted green color brightened his hazel eyes.

This morning when he'd come downstairs and watched her do her exercises, she'd had a hard time concentrating, because she'd only wanted to stop and stare at him like a hormone-driven teen.

She swallowed back the urge to throw her arms around him and welcome him home the way a wife would. She wasn't his wife. The hope that one day she might be his wife made her smile. "Hello."

He stared at her in silence as if he couldn't quite believe what he was seeing. "Hello," he said, his tone cautious.

Had her expression given away her thoughts? She

schooled her features to impassive politeness. She'd have to tread slowly with him. Let him get used to the idea of having her around. "Dinner's ready when you are."

He glanced around. "Wow, great." He hesitated, then moved farther into the room, closer to Rachel. So close that she could feel heat radiating from his big body.

"Where's your dad?"

His expression darkened. "He's staying at the station."

Though she didn't comment, she had a feeling she knew why Rod had stayed away. She smiled inwardly and reached to take Josh's jacket from him.

Their hands brushed, electricity shooting through her. Her gaze flew to his. He regarded her warily, his gaze searching her face.

She blinked and stepped back. *Slowly, remember. Don't spook him.* If lightly touching his hand put him on guard, what would an all-out kissing assault do?

She fought back an uncharacteristic giggle tickling her throat. Assaulting a man with her kisses. That was so unlike her. But this wasn't just any man. This was Josh. What would he do if she kissed him again? Her blood sizzled with anticipation. She just might have to find out.

"This is awesome, Rachel," Griff exclaimed around a mouthful of chocolate brownie.

Josh watched his son with relief. He loved seeing the life shining from Griff's gaze. The ugly dark lump on Griff's forehead reminded Josh the situation could have been much worse.

And he was thankful for Rachel's stoic presence.

Her ability to remain calm, to think in the midst of a crisis. Her willingness to stay with Griff, despite Josh's objections. She touched Josh deeply.

"Would you like another, Josh?" Rachel asked, her voice smooth and satiny.

She held out the pan, her smile pleasant and her eyes amiable. She was a confusing mix of cold and hot.

When she'd first come back to town, he'd have sworn there was no heat in the perfectly sculptured icehouse surrounding her. But he'd seen glimpses of the woman beneath the ice, a woman who was open and friendly, gracious and kind. He didn't know what to make of the contrasting elements of Rachel. He looked at the chocolate concoction. "No, thank you. Three's more than enough."

"They met with your approval?"

"Yes." Was she fishing for a compliment? Interesting. "You're a wonderful cook."

A soft hue of pink touched her cheeks. She looked pleased.

Griff chimed in. "This is great, huh, Dad? Wouldn't it be great to have Rachel here all the time?"

Josh's heart dropped to his toes. This was what he'd been afraid of. That his son would get ideas, get more attached. "Son, this has been nice. But Rachel's life's in Chicago. She'll be returning tomorrow or the next day."

Griff scrunched up his face. "Why?"

"The fire will be under control and Grandpa and I will be able to come home."

Griff shook his head. "No. Why does her life have to be there? Why can't it be here?"

Groaning inwardly, Josh glanced at Rachel. Why wasn't she helping him out with this? She'd gone motionless, her expression rigid and frosty. He frowned and turned back to his son. "Griff, Rachel's a doctor in Chicago."

"She could be a doctor here," Griff insisted.

Josh gritted his teeth. "Griff—"

"Couldn't you, Rachel? Couldn't you be a doctor here? Couldn't you live here with us? We could be a family," Griff implored, his eyes shining with unshed tears.

Josh clenched his fists. His son's heart was going to be broken. Anger—at himself for allowing this and at Rachel for wheedling her way into their lives—made his pulse pound.

And still she sat there cold as ice. Unfeeling and uncaring that she was destroying his son's young heart. He didn't even want to think about his own heart. Right now all that mattered was Griff. Josh needed to do damage control. "Son, please. Let's talk late—"

Then she moved, cutting off what he was about to say.

She leaned forward, her hand reaching to Griff. His son clung to her. Her expression was no less icy, but sparks of heat danced just beyond the cold. Would he ever be able to figure her out? "Griff, I'd love to stay. But that's something your father and I need to discuss."

Floored, Josh sat back in his chair. She had no right to get his son's hopes up. No right to suggest there was some way for them. What about her precious career? What about her life in Chicago? He couldn't allow himself to give in to the spurt of hope her words produced.

If he did, he'd never recover.

Enraged by Rachel's suggestive remark, Josh abruptly stood. "Griff, this is something we'll discuss later. Right now you need your rest."

"Aw, Dad," Griff complained, his gaze darting between the two adults.

"Go on, Griff. Your dad's right."

Josh couldn't look at Rachel. He had to concentrate on his son. Had to get him out of there to a safer place. He picked Griff up and strode from the room.

"Dad, are you angry?"

Trying to control the wrath raging in his heart, Josh said carefully, "I'm upset."

"Why?"

Climbing the stairs, Josh wondered how best to answer that question. He decided on the direct and honest approach. "Because I'd like Rachel to stay, too, but she can't. She's a doctor and that will always be her priority."

Griff frowned, seeming to think over his father's words. "But she could be a doctor and still be in our family. Kevin's mom's a lawyer and she's still part of their family."

"That's different," he responded through a throat tight with aching. He ached for his son, for himself. He ached because he didn't want Rachel to leave.

But she couldn't stay. He couldn't play second fiddle to her career, knowing one day she might decide she no longer wanted to do both. And he'd be the one she'd give up.

He laid Griff on his bed.

Griff settled himself back on the pillow. "Why's that different?"

Josh sighed. "Because it just is. Rachel lives in the big city. She'd never be content here."

"Sure she would."

"But that's not what I want," Josh said harshly. He smoothed hair back from Griff's bruise, careful not to put pressure on the lump. "If I remarry, I want someone who would be content to be my wife and your mother."

Griff stared at him for a long moment, then his little jaw set into a determined line. "When I get married, my wife can be anything she wants to be."

Griff's simple, profound statement hit Josh hard, knocking the breath from his lungs.

He realized it wasn't about Rachel's career choice. It wouldn't have mattered if she'd become a dentist, a teacher or an accountant. As long as her career, her dream, was more important than his love, he couldn't risk his heart. He couldn't measure her commitment to him and he needed concrete assurance.

Josh gathered his son close to his chest. "I love you, Griff."

"I love you, too, Dad."

He left Griff with the bedside lamp on and books to read.

Squaring his shoulders, Josh knew what he had to do. It was time to tell Rachel to leave. Not tomorrow, or the next day, but now. Her presence was too confusing, too painful. For both Griff and himself. He was tired of hurting, tired of feeling that ache take root in his soul.

The healing process would take time, but he would

heal. They would heal together, he and his son. They didn't need Rachel.

The thought left him feeling cold and empty, reassuring him that he was making the right choice. Because without Rachel in his life, he would be empty and cold.

He stepped into the kitchen to see Rachel holding the phone receiver to her ear. She had her back to him, with one finger she traced patterns in the woodwork on the wall.

"Yes, of course. I do realize the importance of my position and I'll be back to…I understand, Doctor. Yes, I will take care of the situation. A few days at the most."

Josh didn't need any further confirmation that sending Rachel away now was the right thing to do. He and his son couldn't withstand the torture of having her around for a few more days.

A noise behind Rachel announced Josh's presence. She turned in time to see him stalking away. She finished her call and hung up.

With a sigh she leaned against the wall. The chief of staff of Cook County Hospital in Chicago wanted to know when she would be returning. She'd bought some time because she needed time to sort out the future, but she also knew she had a responsibility to the hospital. She would go back to resign and help make the transition easier for a new attending.

But right now finding Josh was more important.

She hesitated before stepping into the living room. She was in trouble. This confrontation had come faster than she had wanted or expected. But life always worked out the way it did for a reason. God was in control and if His plan was for them to have this out now, she'd meet the challenge head-on. As always.

Logical and sound reasoning. Challenging questions. Unemotional. Those were the buzzwords that she had to remember. Now to keep her emotions in check and give Josh a rational argument for why they could work, why she could now stay in Sonora and be a doctor here. Why she could be his wife.

If only she had done some research by calling a female colleague and finding out how she managed to raise a family and be an effective doctor. No matter. She was going into this discussion armed with her love and force of will as her weapons. She had to convince Josh that she could be wife, mother *and* doctor.

Tread slowly.

A wild thought ran through her mind. She wanted to kiss him. Wanted to touch him, feel the connection to him she felt every time they touched. She shook her head. That approach wouldn't work. She almost giggled again, thinking how he'd reacted in the kitchen by the mere brushing of their hands. No, coming in with lips blazing wouldn't be the best way to start what was going to be a draining and lengthy discussion.

Drawing herself up and taking a fortifying breath, she sedately glided into the room and stopped at the end of the couch. Josh sat with his long legs stretched out in front of him and his big body taking up one end of the couch.

How to begin? "I think your son and your father have been doing a little matchmaking," she stated quietly.

He laughed slightly. "You just now noticed?"

A wry smile touched her lips. "I suspected it. I suspected Rod and Mom G. were up to something, but I was surprised by Griff's manipulations. He's a smart boy."

"Too smart for his own good."

She wondered what they'd discussed when he'd carried Griff upstairs. "I hope you weren't too hard on him for trying to bring us together."

He stared at her through hooded eyes. "I don't want him to get hurt," he stated flatly.

"Then maybe we should discuss his suggestion." Her voice sounded even, but inside she quivered with hope and dread. Hope that he'd want her love, dread that he wouldn't. Hope that they'd find a way to make them a family, dread that logic and reasoning wouldn't work.

He regarded her steadily. "Discuss?"

"Yes." She sat on the couch, keeping a safe distance away. If she touched him, she wouldn't be able to keep her emotions from showing.

"All right. Let's discuss. What kind of game are you playing?" His voice was low and tinged with a sharp edge.

"There's no game." She understood his confusion. Her own awakening needs and feelings bemused her.

"Rachel, you can't waltz into our lives, getting our hopes up when you have no intention of staying."

The indefinable undertone to his words prepared her for battle. She jumped into the fray with both feet. "I could see myself staying here."

A tawny brow rose. "Oh?"

"I mean..." What did she mean? How did she express the contentment she'd felt the past two days? How did she express the love expanding in her heart?

How did she stay unemotional when she wanted to throw herself in his arms and declare her love and ask him to love her back?

She drew herself up, collecting her composure. "I mean, I've enjoyed being here. I've enjoyed caring for your son." She swallowed then went on steadily. "I've enjoyed caring for you."

In the waning light of evening, his hazel eyes searched her face.

She rushed on. "Twelve years ago we were both young and we loved each other with an immature love. Neither of us was willing to compromise. We both dug in our heels and hurt each other."

His expression intensified, laying claim to her heart. "We did hurt each other. And I'm sorry for that."

"Me, too." She clasped her hands together to keep from reaching out to him. "We're older now, more mature. We've had time to learn to compromise. We've had time to figure out what we want in life."

She paused and drew strength from the conviction in her heart. "I know what I want in life, Josh. I want you." She gestured with her hand, encompassing the house. "I want this. I love you, Josh. Do you think you could love me?"

Chapter Sixteen

The heat in his gaze threatened to scorch, to enflame Rachel beyond endurance.

"Loving you, Rachel, was never the problem."

He loved her. She couldn't breathe for the joy bubbling in her heart. She trembled with the effort to contain her emotion. "You're right, love wasn't the problem. It was us. We each had set ideas of how we wanted our lives. I needed to be a doctor."

"And I've always wanted a wife who'd be passionate about me, about our life together."

"You could have that, Josh. With me."

"Could I?" His gaze narrowed and one corner of his mouth curved with cynicism. "What happened to 'my career's my priority. God wants me to make a difference'?"

Being slapped with her own words popped her little bubbles of joy. "I do believe God wants me to make a difference and my career *has* been my priority."

"So, you've had a miraculous change of heart?"

She stiffened. *Stay unemotional.* "In a way. God

has been working on me ever since I returned home.'' If Josh heard the hitch in her voice as she said the last word he didn't indicate it. She swallowed, stunned to realize she was indeed home.

''Right. And how long will playing house be enough for you?''

''That's not fair, Josh.''

''No, it's not fair. Life's not fair. But then again God never promised life would be fair.''

The bitterness in his voice made her cringe. How could she get through to him? ''These past few days here have made me realize that I've been too...'' She trailed off, searching for the right word.

''Obsessed?''

She frowned. ''No. Focused.''

''And just where's the line, Rachel?''

''Line?''

''The line between doing God's will and obsession?''

She bit back her stirring anger. ''I haven't been obsessed. I've been committed and focused.''

He stood and moved to the fireplace. For a long moment he stared into the empty grate. Finally he pivoted, his gaze riveting. ''What drives you, Rachel?''

Her mother's lifeless body flashed across the screen in her mind. Gut-wrenching pain followed the image. Her instinctive reaction was to push the pain to the far corners of her soul, but the need to tell him stopped her.

Maybe if she spoke of her mother's death, he'd finally understand. Mustering every ounce of courage she possessed, she rose. ''Do you really want to know?''

He folded his arms across his chest as if to protect himself from her. "Yes, I do."

Rachel swallowed several times before she could find her voice. "I was six when my mother died."

His expression softened. "I know. She died of a heart condition."

"She did have a heart condition when she died, but that wasn't what killed her."

"What do you mean?"

Rachel took a deep breath and slowly exhaled, careful to keep her voice unemotional. "She'd been under a doctor's care for a long time. Some days she was bedridden, other days she was like everyone else's mom. Normal." She stared out the window, her gaze trained on the big oak tree with the swing. She remembered the heat of that summer's day and the fear. "Mom was having a good day. We'd been shopping for school clothes when she started having trouble breathing."

Her chest grew heavy with remembered panic; she fought against letting the memory affect her. "We'd hurried from the store, our purchases forgotten. Mom drove, weaving all over the road and I was so scared we'd have an accident. We arrived at the hospital in one piece. The orderlies took her away. A nurse led me to a waiting area." She closed her eyes, unsure if she could tell the rest.

Josh moved, his warm hand covered hers. "Rachel, if it's too painful you don't have to tell me."

His compassion gave her the strength to continue. "I need to tell you." She squeezed his hand. "To make you understand. I saw her, Josh. Lying on the table so still and pale. Machines screaming, the doctors frantic.'' The horror of the day haunted her dreams.

''Her heart failed,'' Josh stated, as if that explained everything.

''No,'' she cried. ''Her heart didn't just fail, the doctors failed.''

''Rachel, you of all people should know life's uncertain. Your mother had a bad heart and she died from it.''

She yanked her hand from his grip. She'd heard those words before. The doctors, the social workers, her shrink. Useless anger dripped from her words. ''You sound like everyone else. My whole life people have tried to make me believe that lie, but I know what happened.''

''What did happen?''

She clenched her fists. Hating the anger and bitterness roaring to life again. ''When the nurse wasn't looking, I went into the room. I saw them. I heard the doctor's words. He'd said, 'This shouldn't have happened.'''

''What shouldn't have happened?''

Rachel drew herself up. ''Whatever mistake cost my mother her life.''

''Do you have proof that they made a mistake?'' he asked gently.

''I have my memory.'' It was all the proof she needed.

Josh laid a hand on her arm. ''The memory of a scared six-year-old.''

''Don't patronize me, Josh.''

''I'm not. It's sad to think you've carried this burden with you your whole life. Why didn't you ever tell me?''

Lifting one stiff shoulder was all she could manage. "I tried. Your knowing wouldn't have changed anything. I still would have left to become a doctor."

"Yeah, but at least it wouldn't have hurt so bad." His expression turned rife with contrition. "Maybe I would've…"

"Waited?" Tears of regret stung her eyes. "I'm sorry, Josh. I was young and focused on my goal. We can't torture ourselves with what ifs. All that matters now is the future. Our future. Do you understand now why I had to become a doctor? Why making a difference was so important? I wanted to save others from the pain and rage of knowing a mistake cost them the life of their loved one."

"Yes, I understand." He backed away, the physical distance not nearly as wide as the emotional distance he'd just created.

His glittering hazel eyes bore into her. "But you have to understand where *I'm* coming from, what *I* need. Apparently we both have mother issues. The day I watched my mother walk away from her family to pursue her dream, I swore I wouldn't settle for less than a woman who would put her family first."

She closed her eyes, her heart screaming in agony over his loss. "You wouldn't have to settle for less, Josh. Not with me. Not ever. Don't you know that?"

"No. I don't." His tone was as coarse as sandpaper. "I don't know that one day you won't decide you've made a mistake. Decide that life wasn't fulfilling enough here. That I wasn't enough."

Her chest threatened to crack wide open. "That wouldn't happen."

"Dad didn't think it would happen, either. He tried to keep her, promised her anything if she'd stay. But she couldn't do both. She wanted her art more than she wanted us. She loved her art more than she loved her son.''

The hurt so evident in his eyes tore at her soul. She reached out a hand. "I'm sure that's not true."

He jerked away. "Why weren't we enough for her?"

Behind the handsome exterior, she glimpsed the little boy who hurt with unspeakable torment. His mother's bitter betrayal had scarred the boy and the man. Her heart broke right down the middle, the two sides twisting in anguish. "I don't have an answer to that."

His eyes closed as if the pain were too excruciating. "I don't want to be hurt again, and I don't want my son hurt. I can't have you in our lives if we aren't your priority."

She stared up at him, tears filling her eyes. His words about Andrea came rushing back: *If I'd loved her enough. Been enough.* Josh took the weight of the world upon his broad shoulders, hefted the responsibility for other people like a heavy cloak. She'd thought he'd been wallowing in self-pity when he'd made that statement, but now she realized he owned the sentiment. "Not enough" was branded across his heart by his own hand.

He had no idea how much more than enough he was. *Dear Lord, I don't know how to reach him.*

Digging deep for her last vestige of strength and courage to do the one thing she hated most, she laid her heart and her emotions bare, vulnerable and exposed, before this wonderful man whom she loved with every fiber of her being. "I am who I am, Josh. A woman who loves you, wants to be with you and who's also a doctor. You can't ask me to give up a part of myself.

"God gave me a gift to heal people. I'm good at what I do. I find great satisfaction in my work. But I believe God has been trying to teach me that there can be more. If you take me, you take the whole package. I'm not saying it'll be easy, but if we work together, we can find a way. In time we'll both adjust."

His expression was heartbreaking in its intensity. He seemed to consider her words; conflicting emotions played across the hard planes of his face. Finally he shook his head. "I can't, Rachel. I can't take the risk. I don't have it in me."

Anguish, deep and exploding, nearly sent her to her knees. She gathered her control tightly, taking the composure that had served her so well over the years and wrapping it around her like cocoon. "A wise woman once told me that happiness lies beyond what you think's possible. You only have to have enough faith. God will take care of the rest."

A spasm of regret crossed his face. "I have plenty of faith in God. It's me I don't have faith in."

"Oh, Josh."

He stepped back, away from her outstretched hand. "It won't work, Rachel. I don't ever want to feel that way again."

Her hand dropped to her side. A spurt of anger gripped her. "So you'd rather be alone than take a chance on me?"

"That's the way it has to be. It would be best if you left as soon as you can." He walked past her and out the front door.

A scream of soul-searing pain tore at Rachel's insides as she watched him disappear into the night. Her legs could no longer hold her upright; she slowly sank to the floor.

Raw and bleeding inside, Rachel fought against despair. They would never find a way together if he wasn't willing to fight for it.

God, tell me what to do.

How could Josh think he wasn't enough? Enough for what? Her? Did he not trust her that much? Her mouth twisted wryly. *What have I done to earn that trust? Except lay my love down like a gauntlet, daring him to pick it up.*

Loving you, Rachel, was never the problem.

A spark of hope leapt to life. He loved her, even if he didn't want to admit it. He just didn't trust her not to break his heart.

His mother's betrayal had damaged Josh's perceptions and his ability to trust with faith. What could she do to rebuild that trust? To build his faith in her?

The answer that roared to her mind sent her doubling over. She couldn't defame her mother's memory; she couldn't give up medicine. Being a doctor defined her, made her who she was. If she walked away from that, what would be left?

Josh's wife.

A woman of faith.

Lord, what do I do? I thought You were giving us a second chance.

Understanding flooded her mind and a gentle peace settled over her.

"I do trust you, Lord." She spoke softly, reverently. "I want both. But if I have to choose, this time I choose Josh."

* * *

Josh stared at the moon's reflection wavering in the pool's water. He felt like such a fool. Rachel had offered him his heart's desire—her love—and he'd walked away. He loved her and she loved him. Why couldn't that be enough?

Because deep inside, fear laid claim to his heart.

Fear that his love wouldn't be enough. Fear that Rachel would one day walk away like his mother had. Fear that he couldn't survive her departure from his life.

Father, why am I so consumed with fear?

He closed his eyes with weary pain. Fear wasn't of God. God was love and light and hope. And yet, fear twisted in his heart.

Rachel's words floated back to him on the evening breeze.

A wise woman once told me that happiness lies beyond what you think's possible. You only have to have enough faith. God will take care of the rest.

Faith. It all came down to faith. Faith in God, faith in himself and faith in Rachel.

Faith's being sure of what we hope for and certain of what we do not see.

"God, forgive me for not having enough faith in You. Please, Lord, take my fear." He whispered his plea to the night sky.

"Josh?" Rachel approached and stopped beside him.

He stiffened, bracing himself for her goodbye. He didn't want her to say goodbye. But he wasn't free of the fear. A touch, like the delicate kiss of a snowflake on his arm, drew his attention.

"Are you okay?"

Rachel's sweet voice, so full of concern, wrapped

around him. He tried to speak, to say he wasn't okay, he'd never be okay without her, but the constriction of his throat muscles wouldn't allow sound to travel from his body.

She withdrew her hand. "I'm not going to let you do this," she said. Her voice now held an edge of steel.

He looked at her. In the moonlight shining on her beautiful face he could see traces of her tears. Tenderness filled him, crowding the fear until he thought he'd choke on it. She'd cried because of him. He didn't want to make her cry, didn't want to hurt her. He loved her.

Her voice softened. "You're so full of anger and hurt. I can understand why you're afraid to trust me, to trust anyone. What your mother did was wrong. She shouldn't have abandoned you. But she made a choice and you have to live with the result of that choice.

"Now *you* have a choice, Josh. You can choose to hold on to the bitterness and the pain or you can forgive her."

He drew back. Something ugly and hateful twisted in his soul. "For...give her?" He could barely get the words out. "You want me to condone what she did?"

Compassion and sadness filled her eyes, lighting the blue depths like beacons in the night. "Not condone her actions, *forgive* her actions. Those are two very different things."

"No, they're not. Not in my book."

"In God's book they are."

"How can you say that?"

Her eyes narrowed slightly. "Do you believe the Bible is truth?"

"Of course," he said indignantly.

"Do you believe that your sins are forgiven?"

"Yes." He snapped the word.

"We need to work on your perceptions," she stated quietly.

"What are you talking about?"

"Do you think that when God forgives you He says, 'that's okay. I know you didn't mean it. Go back to what you were doing'?"

He frowned. What she said didn't seem right, yet wasn't that forgiveness? "I don't know. I think so."

A sweet smiled touched her lips. "When God forgives, He takes our sin and removes it as far as the east is from the west. Then He expects us to move on with our life, not looking back and *not* repeating the sin. He also demands that we forgive those who've sinned against us."

He blinked, trying to wrap his mind around her words. "But how do I forgive her? I don't even know where she is."

"Oh, Josh. She doesn't have to know." She moved closer, her slender hand taking his, the gesture unbearably kind. "When God forgives, it's for us. When we forgive, it's for God. Forgiveness frees us to have a relationship with God and…with others."

"Frees us?" Could what she said be that simple and so hard all at once?

"It'll take time. I'm not saying that if you say you forgive her you'll magically be healed. But have faith in God. Pray for your mother, pray for the strength to forgive. In time the little boy inside of you—" she placed her hand over his heart "—he will be able to let go of the awful stuff. And you, the man, will be able to trust and love.''

Josh's mind resisted; the pain was too much a part of him to believe it could be so easily set aside. Thinking of her anger and bitterness toward those she held responsible for her mother's death, he asked, ''Have you forgiven the doctors?''

There was a softening in her eyes. ''I'm beginning to, thanks to you.''

''Me?''

''My mother died in the E.R. at Sonora Community. And until two days ago, I'd never set foot back in there. I didn't believe I ever could. That's why I'd never wanted to practice medicine in Sonora.''

Her softly spoken words floored him. He'd never made the connection, never realized the depth of her pain. ''I'm so sorry, Rachel. I never...'' He widened his eyes as a horrible thought occurred to him. ''I asked you to go in there.''

She nodded, a confident smile playing at her mouth. ''Yes, you did, and I'm grateful. Because if you hadn't, I would have never known that my life's work had made a difference, that my mother hadn't died in vain. I've faced my demons and have been set free. I want the same for you, Josh. You will find freedom in forgiveness.''

Pride for the woman she'd become filled him, restricting his breathing. He thought over her words. Could forgiveness release the fear? Could he learn to love without being afraid to lose that love? ''I don't know if I can, Rachel.''

Her gaze seemed to frost over, like the car windshield after a winter's night. ''Do you love me, Josh?''

She took a few steps away. Suddenly she was distant and untouchable again. She kept doing that, hiding behind an icy wall.

He realized with a start that *was* what she was doing. Hiding.

All the times he'd thought her cold and unfeeling, she'd been hiding. Hiding emotions that made her vulnerable. Hiding her feelings from him.

Inside the wondrously beautiful ice sculpture was a warm and loving woman waiting to be freed.

In forgiveness there was freedom, she said. Could he forgive his mother? Could he forgive God for allowing his mother to do what she'd done? His throat worked and his eyes burned as it dawned on him that deep down he blamed God for his mother leaving. *Oh, Lord, forgive me for blaming You.*

He gives us free will, Rachel had told him.

His mother made her choice. Josh now faced a choice to forgive and move on. His father had loved his mother enough to let her go. Josh hadn't understood until now how much courage that had taken. Did he have enough courage, enough love to let Rachel stay?

"Josh, I love you."

Rachel's tender words brought him out of his thoughts. She was so beautiful, standing there bathed in the full moon's brilliance. Light reflected off her dark hair, creating a shimmering glow that surrounded her. Her blue eyes were big and bright and cool with emotion. He'd been thickheaded not to realize before that when she was her coldest was when she was feeling the most.

She pulled in a breath. "I want to build a life with you. I want to earn your trust, make you know in your soul that I would never break my commitment to you. Love's a choice, Josh. Every day, it's a choice we have to make.'' Her voice echoed across the pool water, sounding brittle and frozen. ''I choose you, Josh. And if giving up medicine's what it takes, I will.''

''You'd hate that, Rachel. And then you'd end up hating me.'' He scrubbed a hand over his face. ''I wish there were some way to measure commitment.''

''The only measurable thing I can do to prove my love for you is to give up medicine.''

Her words, so at odds with her icy tone, stopped his breath, trapping the air around his heart until he thought he'd pass out for lack of oxygen. She'd give up being a doctor for him. She'd make the ultimate sacrifice as a testament to her love.

He searched his heart, going over the things she'd said. Love was a choice to be made every day. Forgiveness brought freedom. Faith was believing and trusting in something you couldn't see but knew to be true anyway.

For him to find happiness, he had to step out in faith and trust Rachel.

In two long strides he closed the distance between them and took her in his arms. Her body felt rigid and straight in his hands. ''Aw, Rachel. It's too much.''

She tilted her head to look up at him. Her eyes glittered like icicles. ''What?''

A slow, sweeping joy filled him. He breathed deep of the love at his fingertips. ''It's too much, but more than enough.''

She went impossibly colder.

A smile gathered at the corners of his mouth.

Her gaze narrowed. He felt the touch of frostbite and didn't mind.

"Why are you looking at me like a cat when he finds the key to a birdcage?"

His smile grew, and love, perfect love, drove out the fear. He caressed her cheek. "I'm smiling because I love you. And I won't let you give up being a doctor."

"You do? You won't?"

"Yes, I do. And no, I won't. You are who you are, Rachel. And I love every inch of you the way you are."

She blinked rapidly, but tears fell from her eyes anyway. The cold receded and a warm front moved in. "I promise you, Josh. You will always come first."

"I'll hold you to that promise," he said as his mouth moved closer, hovering, waiting.

She went on tiptoe and closed the distance into a heart-stopping, mind-melting kiss.

"Rachel," he said against her mouth.

"Hmm?"

"I'll need lots of these."

"Kisses of assurance," she stated huskily and recaptured his mouth.

"Rachel?"

"Hmm?"

"Will you marry me?"

She stilled, her lips turning cool against his mouth, her breath hitched. Then slowly the essence of Rachel fanned out around him, enflaming them both. Her head tilted back and indescribable joy reflected in her gaze. "Yes. I'll marry you. Only you."

Epilogue

Josh followed Griff through the double sliding-glass doors of Sonora Community Hospital's emergency entrance. Rachel stood behind the administration desk, her dark hair pulled back in a simple ponytail that brushed across the shoulders of her white coat.

"Hi, Mom," Griff called out as they approached.

She looked up from the report in her hand. Her eyes crinkled at the corners and her mouth curved upward into a welcoming smile that never ceased to move Josh deep down in his soul. Quickly she laid the file down before moving around the desk. Taking Griff in her arms, she held him close, as close as her protruding stomach would allow.

"How's she doing today?" Griff asked before kissing the mound that held his baby sister.

"Kicking up a storm," she commented, and met Josh's gaze.

The tender love in her blue gaze stirred his blood, stoking the fire that always burned for his wife. In almost two years of marriage, the love between them grew more intense very day. "Are you ready for lunch?"

She hesitated. Old apprehension surfaced, catching him off guard. But he quickly squelched it. They both had lives outside of each other.

He was so proud of her and he respected the importance of the work she did. He could see the differences she made and knew about the lives she'd touched. And she supported his career, never once making him feel guilty for the time he put into the forestry service. They both carried the weight of responsibility on their shoulders, but as a couple, as a family, they would always come first.

Together, their love was enough.

"A quick lunch, if I want to get out of here early today to watch Griff's baseball game."

"Done." Easy contentment and satisfaction filled him. As they left the hospital, Griff skipping on ahead and their baby girl thriving beneath Rachel's heart, Josh sent up a prayer of thanks for bringing love back into his life.

* * * * *

Dear Reader,

I hope you enjoyed my first book with Steeple Hill. I'm very excited to be able to share Josh and Rachel's story with you. These two have been talking to me for a very long time now. They had to learn the power and freedom of forgiveness in order to find their way to a deep and lasting love. A love worth fighting for.

I used my childhood memories of Sonora as well as some creative license in constructing the backdrop for this story. If you ever get a chance to visit the gold counties of the Sierra Nevada, make sure you visit historic Columbia. I know you'll grow as fond of the area as I am.

May God bless you always.

Terri Reed

Love Inspired®

MIXED
BLESSINGS

BY

CATHY MARIE
HAKE

It was a mother's worst nightmare: widowed
Marie Cadant was told the little boy she loved was
not the child she'd given birth to. And single parent
Peter Hallock, the man who had her biological son, was
determined to keep both boys. Uniting their families in a
marriage of convenience seemed the only option, and
tying the knot easy enough. But now Peter had to convince
Marie that their marriage was truly made in heaven!

Don't miss
MIXED BLESSINGS
on sale July 2004

Available at your favorite retail outlet.

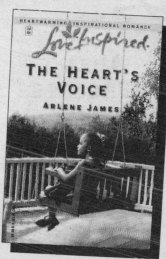

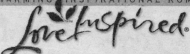
In July look for
Adam's Promise,
the first title in
the dramatic
six-book romantic
suspense series

Faith
On The Line

LoveInspired

In July look for
Adam's Promise,
the first title in
the dramatic
six-book romantic
suspense series

Faith
On The Line

ADAM'S PROMISE

GAIL GAYMER MARTIN